D1505145

The Third Door

EMILY RODDA

PUFFIN
an imprint of Penguin Canada Books Inc.

Published by the Penguin Group
Penguin Canada Books Inc., 90 Eglinton Avenue East, Suite 700, Toronto, Ontario, Canada M4P 2Y3

Penguin Group (USA) Inc., 375 Hudson Street, New York, New York 10014, U.S.A.
Penguin Books Ltd, 80 Strand, London WC2R 0RL, England
Penguin Ireland, 25 St Stephen's Green, Dublin 2, Ireland (a division of Penguin Books Ltd)
Penguin Group (Australia), 707 Collins Street, Melbourne, Victoria 3008, Australia
(a division of Pearson Australia Group Pty Ltd)
Penguin Books India Pvt Ltd, 11 Community Centre, Panchsheel Park, New Delhi – 110 017, India
Penguin Group (NZ), 67 Apollo Drive, Rosedale, Auckland 0632, New Zealand
(a division of Pearson New Zealand Ltd)
Penguin Books (South Africa) (Pty) Ltd, 24 Sturdee Avenue, Rosebank, Johannesburg 2196, South Africa

Penguin Books Ltd, Registered Offices: 80 Strand, London WC2R 0RL, England

Published in Puffin hardcover by Penguin Canada, 2013
Simultaneously published in the United States by Scholastic Press, an imprint of Scholastic Inc.

1 2 3 4 5 6 7 8 9 10 (RRD)

Text and graphics copyright © Emily Rodda, 2012

*Publisher's note: This book is a work of fiction. Names, characters, places and incidents
either are the product of the author's imagination or are used fictitiously, and any resemblance
to actual persons living or dead, events, or locales is entirely coincidental.*

The text was set in Palatino.
Book design by Elizabeth B. Parisi

Manufactured in the U.S.A.

LIBRARY AND ARCHIVES CANADA CATALOGUING IN PUBLICATION

Rodda, Emily, author
The third door / Emily Rodda.

(The three doors trilogy ; book 3)
ISBN 978-0-670-06653-7 (bound)

I. Title. II. Series: Rodda, Emily Three doors trilogy ; book 3.

PZ7.R6275Thi 2013   j823'.914   C2013-905034-5

Visit the Penguin Canada website at **www.penguin.ca**

Special and corporate bulk purchase rates available; please see
www.penguin.ca/corporatesales or call 1-800-810-3104, ext. 2477.

CONTENTS

THE SALTINGS

It was past midnight, but no one slept inside the stronghold of the Master. The day just ended had been eagerly awaited, but instead of triumph it had brought disaster. The Master's rage had been terrible. The gray-faced supervisor now in charge of the vast Harbor complex had decreed that there was to be no rest until every room had been restored to order.

The flooded basement had been partly drained, but the workers there still toiled knee-deep in oily water thick with drowned slays. Surveying the bloated bodies of the ferocious beasts she had bred from far less dangerous stock, the supervisor felt no emotion. That was not surprising. She was no more human than the gray-clad guards laboring around her. Like them, she existed only to serve.

She was already calculating how long it would be until she could begin the breeding program again with the handful of slays she had left. She was also deciding that very large quantities of the red substance known as jell would speed the process. The slaves in the Diggings would have to work harder.

It did not occur to her to wonder why the Shadow Lord, who had such powerful sorcery at his command, required an army of deadly flying beasts that could attack by day as well as by night. It was not in her nature to ask such questions. What the Master wanted he must have — that was all that mattered.

The thing he wanted most at present was the capture of the four enemy spies who had dared to interfere with his plans. It had been early morning when the spies fled the Harbor, leaving havoc behind them, but the supervisor had no doubt they would be caught, even after so long a delay.

Soon the Master's giant birds would recover from the feeding frenzy that had left them gorged and unable to fly. At daybreak, they would be released to hunt the criminals down.

The prisoners the spies had saved would go free. By now, they would have scattered, and with Slave Hunter Kyte dead, there was no one to identify them. Mine rats all looked the same to the supervisor and to most of the other workers in the Harbor.

The four spies were different. They would be easy to recognize. They were well fed, and two of them were copper-heads. They had the means to make themselves invisible, certainly. But the birds were the

Master's creatures, not natural beasts like slays, and the Master's power would sharpen their eyes.

The spies could not remain hidden forever. There would be no escape for them.

✳

Rye, Sonia, Dirk, and Sholto were at that very moment trying to prove the supervisor wrong. Hand in hand, sped by Rye's magic ring and invisible beneath Rye's hood, they were gliding over the parched plain called the Scour. The clouded sky was dark, but not so dark that they could not see their way, and thanks to the charmed feather Rye held, their feet did not touch the pebbled track that guided them.

The four had not dared to move in daylight, though Rye and Sonia now had brown hair instead of red, thanks to a dark powder given to them by Cap of the Den, who had taken them into hiding. They had slept through the day in the Den, and even when night fell, they had lingered. They knew that their lanky friend Bones, who had given them such valuable help at the Harbor, would raise an outcry if he saw his "magic ones" leaving him. So they had waited till Bones was as deeply asleep as everyone else in the Den before slipping away.

"It cannot be helped," Sonia whispered, feeling Rye's guilt as they reached the place where they had first seen Bones — the pyramid of stones at the edge of the Saltings wasteland.

Rye sighed. "If only we could have taken Bones

and the others home with us! And Bird and all the people from Nanny's Pride farm, too!"

"I agree," Dirk growled. "But if we are to stay in Weld only briefly, and then see what is beyond the wooden Door, we will have to stay hidden. Bones and the rest would make that impossible."

"Indeed." Sholto grimaced. "Imagine the Warden's panic if he saw a horde from beyond the Wall pouring into the Keep! Faene — that girl you tell me you smuggled in through the golden Door — sounds as if she could pass for a Weld person if she had to. The same cannot be said for Cap's tribe — or Bird's."

Rye knew his brothers were right. The ragged men and women of the Den, wretchedly thin, with wild hair and scarlet jell-stained hands, would seem terrifying to the orderly citizens of Weld. The small, fierce people from Nanny's Pride farm would be almost as frightening.

"And they could not have hidden in the tower with Annocki and Faene," Dirk added. "There would not have been room to move!"

"Who is Annocki?" Sholto asked.

"The Warden's daughter," Dirk said with a grin. "Sonia's friend, and the lady you are to marry, brother, if there is any justice! You were the one who found the enemy of Weld and destroyed the skimmers — the slays, as they call them here. You should win the Warden's prize!"

"Do not be ridiculous!" Sholto snapped. "I have no wish to marry anyone — let alone a woman who has been forced to accept me!"

Sonia shot him an approving glance, but made no comment. "The people here would not follow us through a sorcerer's Door to Weld even if we asked them, Rye," she said instead. "They are terrified of magic — all of them except Bones. They were grateful to us, but still they left us to ourselves as soon as they could."

There was a strange, sad note in her voice. Her face was a pale blur in the dimness as she turned her head to stare over the Saltings. The dark, lumpy ground stretched away as far as the eye could see, so seething with moving snails that it seemed to ripple like water.

Rye tried to send her a message of comfort, but her mind was closed to him. Perhaps, he thought, she was imagining what Cap, Bird, and the others would have felt if they had known that Rye had opened the way for the Master's invasion by causing the death of the tyrant Olt. Sonia had always refused to believe that Olt's power protected Dorne from the Lord of Shadows, but surely she accepted it now.

"We had better get on," Dirk said. "Sholto's trail of pyramids will guide us. As I recall, there are ten in all. The first we found — the one that had the remains of your notebook inside it, brother — is very near the silver Door."

5

"Possibly," Sholto muttered, "but I could not find the Door when I looked. Of course, I was not in my right mind at the time." He had tried to speak lightly, but he looked sick as he stared out at the creeping sea of snails ahead.

Rye and Dirk glanced at each other. Sholto had said very little about what had happened to him before he reached the Harbor, and they had not pressed him. They knew there were huge gaps in his memory, and that this disturbed him greatly.

"I have never felt so despairing," Sholto went on, his voice very low. "I thought I had gone mad. It seemed to me that one moment I was in a cave, in a forest I took to be the Fell Zone, and the next I was in a snail-infested wasteland with my mind like murky soup and only my notebook and lantern to remind me who I was."

"You were enchanted, no doubt," Sonia said calmly.

She shrugged as Sholto's eyebrows shot up. "There are magic beings in the Fell Zone, Sholto. They are called the Fellan. Dirk did not see them when he went through the golden Door, but Rye and I did."

As both his brothers looked at him, Rye nodded, though his skin was prickling. He had sworn never to tell who had given him the little bag of magic powers he wore around his neck, so he had thought it best not to mention the Fellan to Dirk and Sholto at all. It shocked him that Sonia had blurted out the name so heedlessly.

Sholto was digging in his pocket, pulling out the

snail-eaten pieces of his notebook that Rye had given him. He sorted through them, squinting in the gloom. "Your light, Rye!" he said. "Just for a moment."

Rye took the crystal from the bag and let its light fall on the fragment in his brother's hand. His voice rising in excitement, Sholto read the words aloud.

The Watchers were very close today. Time and again I felt their eyes on the back of my neck, but when I turned I could see only trees.

"There!" Sonia crowed. "Your 'Watchers' were the Fellan!"

Sholto looked up. His troubled face had cleared. "I *was* in the Fell Zone, then!" he exclaimed. "I did *not* imagine it!"

"Of course not!" Sonia laughed. "You had only been in the Harbor for a few days when we found you, Sholto. But you have been away from Weld for over a year! Plainly you did not spend all that time in the Saltings — you could not possibly have survived. So you were somewhere else, and the Fell Zone is the most likely place. It fills Dorne's center, after all."

"So . . . I came through the silver Door," Sholto said slowly. "I found my way over the Saltings to the Fell Zone. I stayed in the forest, searching for the source of the skimmers, for over a year, and then —"

"Then for some reason the Fellan drove you back into the Saltings," Sonia finished for him. "And it is not surprising that you remember nothing about it. I daresay they wanted to make sure you did not come back."

"I daresay," Sholto drawled.

"So that is settled," Dirk said, relieved to see Sholto looking and sounding more like himself. "Let us make a start. The journey will not take long. Rye has learned to use the feather much better during our time here."

But he had spoken too soon. After only a few minutes, they were moving no faster than walking pace, and their feet kept brushing the snail-covered rocks. Every time this happened thousands of ravenous snails reared horribly, trying to slide onto their shoes. If it had not been for the protection of the armor shell fixed to Rye's finger, the companions would have been dragged down and reduced to skeletons in minutes.

"By the Wall, Rye, can you go no higher?" Dirk whispered.

"I had forgotten the metal that lies among the rocks here," Rye said shakily. "It is affecting the feather's magic."

And the magic of the armor shell, too, he thought but did not say. He could not help noticing that the snails were not bouncing away from their shoes, but merely failing to get a good grip.

Sholto had plainly seen the same thing. "Use the light, Rye," he urged. "We are far enough into the wasteland by now to risk that. I am sure that it is only because I managed to keep my lantern going that I survived my night here."

Sure enough, though the light of the crystal was far dimmer than usual, it was enough to keep the snails back. The moment the glow hit them they withdrew into their shells and stayed there.

The light made it far easier to pick out Sholto's pyramid trail, too, so the journey became less tense. Progress was still slow, however, and by the time the tenth pile of stones came into view, the sky was beginning to lighten.

"I remember building that pyramid so clearly," Sholto said in a low voice. "Putting stone upon stone, trying not to think of the night that had just passed, fighting the fear that I had lost my mind . . ."

"Do not think of that," Dirk said quickly. "Think of what you and Rye did! Think that, because of you, no skimmers flew over the Wall last night, and the people of Weld slept safely for the first time in years!"

Sholto half smiled, swatting at one of the giant insects that had begun buzzing around in the past few minutes. The creature fell to the ground, and in seconds the snails had made short work of it.

When they reached the pyramid at last, Rye swept the light crystal around.

"The Door is here somewhere," he murmured. "It is concealed, that is all. Sonia, can you see it?"

But Sonia did not answer, and suddenly it came to Rye that she had not spoken for a long time. He turned to her, and with a stab of panic, he saw that her eyes were glazed. He had been depending on Sonia to find the silver Door, as she had found the golden one. He had forgotten how badly the Saltings affected her.

Sonia! he called to her in his mind. *Can you see the Door?*

Slowly, Sonia turned her head. A slight crease appeared between her eyebrows. "Of course," she mumbled, and pointed.

And there, very near, glimmering slightly in the gloom, was the ghostly shape of the silver Door.

Rye gasped with relief, and after a moment, so did Dirk. Sholto, dumbfounded, simply stared.

They floated awkwardly to the Door, which was hovering a little way above the ground and seemed more solid the closer they came to it. Like the golden Door, it had no handle on this side, but Rye had expected that. He fumbled in the brown bag for the charmed key.

"Look at the snails," Dirk muttered uneasily.

Everyone looked around. Every rock in the Saltings was still. The snails had all retreated into their shells.

"They sense that the sun is rising," Sholto said, glancing at the sky. "Make haste, Rye!"

Rye stuffed the red feather and the light crystal back into the brown bag. His feet thudded down onto the snail-covered rocks as he drew out the tiny key and pressed it to the Door.

To his dismay, nothing happened. He tried again, but still the Door did not move.

Sholto cursed under his breath. "The Master's birds!" he hissed.

In terror Rye looked up, following his brother's gaze. Two dark shapes were speeding toward them beneath the red-stained clouds. Between one blink and another, giant wings, snakelike necks, and cruel talons became visible. A harsh screech split the air.

"They have seen us!" Dirk yelled.

"Keep trying, Rye!" Sholto urged. "You must be touching the wrong place!"

"No!" Sonia cried. "Rye, we got through the golden Door without a key. It opened when you ran at it, remember?"

"I cannot see —" Sholto began, but Rye was willing to try anything. He drew back a little, then threw himself heedlessly at the Door.

There was a sound like a clanging gong as his hands, his boots, and the stick in his belt struck the silver surface. And with joy, he saw a strip of blinding white light appear down one side of the Door.

"Hold on to me!" he shouted as the strip widened. "Hold —"

And then they were all tumbling into the light, and the Door was slamming behind them, shutting out the screeches of the diving sky serpents cheated of their prey.

INSIDE

Dazed with relief, Rye sat up. He felt bruised all over, but what did that matter? By a miracle, he, Sonia, Dirk, and Sholto were safe — safe in the Chamber of the Doors.

"What in Weld has happened here?" he heard Dirk ask in a strained voice.

And only then did Rye register that the floor of the chamber was littered with rubble, and the air was thick with dust.

In shocked silence, the companions picked their way to the fireplace, which was overflowing with bricks, broken clay tiles, and chunks of mortar.

Dirk bent and picked up a piece of tile. "This came from the roof," he said grimly. "The roof caved in up above, by the look of things, and falling debris blocked the chimney. It happened not long ago, I would say. The dust still has not settled."

"How —?" Sholto shook his head, frowning in disbelief.

"Skimmers attacked the tower chimney the night before we left," Rye told him. "The damage was mended, but —"

"The Warden was far more concerned with the look of the chimney than with its strength, and no doubt gave his orders accordingly," Sonia said. "The skimmers must have found a weakness. They broke through."

She sounded perfectly calm, but Rye could feel her trembling. In his mind, he could see her ghastly visions of skimmers bursting into the darkened tower room, flapping and shrieking, needle teeth bared. He could hear her silent cries of fear and grief.

Annocki! Oh, Annocki, Annocki!

"It may not be, Sonia," Rye murmured, putting his arm around the girl and trying to shield his own feeling of dread.

"There should have been no skimmer attack in Weld last night," Sholto muttered, rubbing his forehead. "I was told that the skimmers kept on the lower floor of the Harbor building were the only ones in existence."

"Well, that was untrue, it seems," said Dirk. He was turning the fragment of tile over and over in his blunt fingers. His face was ashen. Clearly he was thinking of Faene — beautiful, gentle Faene of Fleet, who had trusted him, who had followed him to Weld, who had agreed to hide in the tower room with Annocki, believing that there she would be safe.

Rye wet his lips. "We cannot know what has happened until we see for ourselves. We must get up to ground level."

"The chimney may be entirely filled with rubble, for all we know," Dirk said heavily, throwing the tile fragment aside. "Clearing it from down here will take days — if we can do it at all."

Rye saw that his brother was not thinking clearly. With his free hand, he felt in the bag hanging around his neck and drew out the light crystal.

"Come on," he urged, turning Sonia away from the fireplace. "Dirk, Sholto — you, too! There is another way out. Have you forgotten how we came into this chamber in the first place?"

Dirk's eyes widened. He swung around, snatched up a broken brick, and charged to the far end of the chamber.

"Ho there!" he bellowed, battering the bare stone wall with the brick. "Guards! Returning volunteers here! Let us in!"

The echoes of his calls rang in the Chamber of the Doors, so that it seemed as if a dozen men were shouting instead of only one. But there was no response from the other side of the wall, and the hard stone surface remained cold and blank.

Dirk spun around as Rye, Sonia, and Sholto joined him. His forehead gleamed with sweat.

14

"I thought we had decided to come and go without being seen," Sholto drawled.

"What does that matter now?" Dirk panted. "We have to find out what has happened!"

"Stand away, Dirk," Rye said quietly. He stepped past his brother and pressed the light crystal to the wall. The dusty stone seemed to dissolve beneath his hand, leaving a clear hole like a window. Through the window, they could all see part of a small round room, its curving walls covered in tiny tiles arranged in swirling patterns of red, yellow, green, and white.

Rye moved the crystal from side to side, but there was nothing more to be seen.

"Where are the guards?" Dirk hissed.

Rye fought down a feeling of dread. The soldiers who guarded the entrance to the Chamber of the Doors would surely not have left their posts except in the case of some truly fearful emergency.

For one thing, a vital part of their duty had to be listening for returning volunteers. There were still some Weld heroes who had not been away long enough to have been declared dead.

His stomach churning, he jerked the crystal away from the wall, and the view of the bare, tiled room winked out. He pushed the crystal into his pocket and drew out the little golden key.

"Take hold of me," he said.

He felt his brothers grip his shoulders. He tightened his arm around Sonia. His heart thudding, he pressed the key to the wall, praying that this time it would work.

Heat shot up his arm like flame. His face burned. Stars danced before his eyes. . . . Then the heat vanished abruptly, and he was sagging against a surface that was smooth and cool on his cheek. He took a deep, shuddering breath. The air that rushed into his lungs was dank, but free of soot and dust.

We are through, he thought.

He opened his watering eyes. The patterns made by the tiny, glittering tiles swirled around him like live things. And suddenly he found that he could see pictures in the patterns. Suddenly he was gazing at banks of ferns and flowers, trees waving in the wind, a bubbling stream. . . .

Wondering, he looked up. Above him arched the blue ceiling, shining like bright sky.

The Sorcerer Dann, Weld's founder, had made this room. These pictures were Dann's visions of the world outside the Wall — the world beyond the golden Door, at least. How he must have missed it! For some reason, an ache rose in Rye's throat, and the vivid images shimmered before his eyes.

"Rye!" Dirk's impatient call shattered the silence. Rye blinked, and the pictures on the walls became meaningless patterns again.

Dirk, Sholto, and Sonia were at the doorway of the little chamber, staring out at the steep, narrow steps that spiraled up through the heart of the Keep. Torches had already sprung into life on the staircase walls, flooding the steps with flickering golden light.

"You go first, Rye," Dirk said, beckoning feverishly. "Keep the key handy. You will need it to open the door into the waiting room."

In single file, the four hurried up the steps, turning and turning again as the staircase wound. Gradually the smells of damp and mold grew fainter. Slowly Rye's skin ceased to prickle as the ancient magic that lingered in the depths of the Keep was left behind.

He could hear the clump of Dirk's boots, and Sholto's labored breathing. But Sonia, who was directly behind him, made no sound at all. Her mind was closed to him. She was quivering with tension.

Rye's journey down these steps with the Warden of Weld had seemed to take a very long time. He vividly remembered feeling that it would never end. So he was startled when, far sooner than he had expected, the steps wound for the last time and he found the way ahead barred by a narrow door.

"We are at the top!" he exclaimed, stopping and dipping into his pocket for the key and the light crystal.

Sonia caught her breath. Rye felt the walls she had raised to guard her thoughts tremble and crack.

Soon I will know. . . . Oh, Annocki . . .

Then Sonia's control broke. All her dammed-up anger and dread, her terrible need to know, burst from her in a mighty wave and crashed into Rye's mind. His hands pressed uselessly to his ringing ears, he lurched forward. The narrow door loomed in front of him. He heard a loud, echoing click. . . .

And the next moment he was stumbling over the long red curtain that had once hidden the door, but now lay tangled underfoot. He kicked himself free, trying to gather his wits. His mind felt bruised. The speed ring was on his finger and the golden key was in his hand, but he could not remember using either of them. He could not even remember the door opening.

But he had to believe the evidence of his own eyes. Dirk and Sholto, looking very startled, were emerging from the stairway and closing the door after them. And he was in the waiting room — the once-elegant waiting room, where dust now hung heavy in the air, curtain rods tilted drunkenly over cracked windows, and rubble spilled from the fireplace.

He pushed the key and the crystal back into the brown bag. After a moment's thought, he did the same with the armor shell. He would not need protection here at home, and the shell would loosen if it sensed he was not in danger. He could not risk its falling off and being lost.

He looked vaguely around for Sonia and caught sight of the table where, not so long ago, he had signed the volunteers' oath of secrecy. Unsteadily, barely aware of what he was doing, he walked to the table and looked down at the clutter that told its own story of sudden alarm.

A scroll crammed with hundreds of signatures, crumpled as if screwed up by furious hands. An unfinished letter in the Warden's small, fussy writing, ending in a blot. A pen that lay where it had fallen. The crystal inkwell overturned, a puddle of ink spreading to stain the white plumes of the Warden's hat.

The first line of the letter caught his eye.

Citizens of Southwall . . .

Southwall, his old home! Why had the Warden been writing to the people of Southwall?

He focused on the words of the letter.

Citizens of Southwall:
Your petition has been received. I must warn you to
abandon your dangerous and unlawful plans at once.
No permit has been given for columns to be built in
Southwall for any purpose. I will consider Healer
Tallus's theory that lighting the night sky will repel
the skimmers at the proper moment. In the meantime,
be assured that the tried and true defenses of silence,
sealed windows and doors, and darkness will make your
families as safe by night as if they were here i̶

"In the *Keep*," Rye heard Sholto drawl behind him. "I daresay the old fool was writing: 'as safe as if they were here in the Keep' when the whole place began crashing down around his ears."

As Rye turned to him, he nodded across the room. "It was a skimmer attack, without doubt," he said soberly. "See for yourself."

Sonia and Dirk were standing by one of the tall windows that lined the wall opposite the fireplace. They did not turn as Rye and Sholto joined them.

Through cracked glass spattered with dust and rain, Rye looked out on a scene of chaos.

The Keep courtyard, misty with drizzle, was heaped with broken stone, shattered glass, smashed roof tiles, and splintered rafters. The ancient bell tree planted by the Sorcerer Dann himself was completely buried.

Confused-looking soldiers, their scarlet leggings streaked with mud, were scooping up rubble and carrying it away in baskets. Keep workers who looked as if they would have been more at home moving official papers from one shelf to another were fluttering around trying to help. Many were in tears.

Hundreds of dead skimmers lay half buried in the mound. Their leathery wings were crushed beneath them. Their terrible claws curved stiffly, jutting into the air. Their pale eyes stared, flooded with blood.

"The tower has fallen, it seems," Dirk said tonelessly. "But it did not drop into the courtyard entirely, by the look of things. The base must have fallen sideways — onto the attic roofs."

"The Keep orphans sleep in the attics." Sonia's voice was as faint as a breath.

Rye took her cold hand. A terrible, helpless rage was burning in his chest. Rage at the tyrant who had sent the skimmers. Rage at the Warden, who in his fever to keep up appearances had failed to protect the most helpless of his people. Rage at himself, for believing that he and his companions had stopped the menace.

He turned to look at the door that led into the grand Keep drawing room. "It may not be as bad as we fear," he said, drawing the hood of concealment over his head. "It may be worse. In any case, there is only one way to find out."

THE LANTERN

Clustered together, hidden from sight by the power of Rye's hood, the four crept through the deserted drawing room. They knew exactly where to go. The moment the heavy waiting room door had cracked open they had heard a dull roar of sound. It was coming from the great hallway that ran the whole length of the Keep.

They had almost reached the hallway door when it burst open. An echoing din of crashes, shouts, groans, and whimpers rolled into the room, and with it came two women in filthy nightgowns. The older of the two had a thin gray braid hanging down her back. The other woman's hair was wound up in dozens of curling rags, so that she looked as if she was wearing a shaggy white cap. The two looked familiar to Rye, but he could not think where he had seen them before.

"Just do what the healer says, Bettina!" the old

woman snapped, seizing an armchair and pushing it back to the nearest wall. "Make as much clear space as you can! And be quick about it! He'll start sending the worst cases in here any minute!"

"The Warden will not like it, Lal," wailed her companion, looking nervously over her shoulder.

"Then the Warden will have to lump it!" the old woman retorted, shoving a dainty little table after the chair and turning to wrestle with a velvet sofa. "Those children need this room more than he does."

Rye suddenly realized why the two looked familiar. They were the kitchen workers he had secretly watched talking to his mother in the Keep kitchen on his last return to Weld. But then they had been wearing starched aprons and prim white caps. No wonder he had not known them at first!

He felt Dirk nudge him and moved cautiously forward. Through the open door, he could see large numbers of people thronging the hallway. Only a few were fully dressed. All looked exhausted, but no one stopped to rest for a moment.

People carrying piles of sheets and towels or hauling buckets brimming with water hurried along on both sides. A long row of small, huddled forms wrapped in blankets occupied the hallway's center strip. Men and women moved quietly along the row, cleaning grime, blood, and tears from young faces, giving water, murmuring comforting words, and even singing lullabies.

A great love for the kind, valiant people of Weld swelled in Rye's chest. A lump rose in his throat.

"They need more healers," Sholto muttered, and darted out into the hallway. "Where is the chief healer?" he snapped at an old man laboring by with two buckets of steaming water.

"The Keep healer is up above, with the orphans who are still trapped," the old man quavered. "But there is another who seems to know what he is doing. Down there, he is, by the door to the Orphans' Stairs. They are bringing the children out that way — lowering them down with ropes, I hear, poor little wretches."

He jerked his head across the hallway, and to the left.

"Thank you!" said Sholto, and instantly he was gone.

"I am sure you would do the same for me," the old man mumbled, and shuffled on.

"The time for hiding is past, I think," Rye said. As Dirk and Sonia nodded tensely, he pulled off the hood.

Dirk dashed from the room with Sonia close behind him. Rye was hard on their heels. Everyone in the hallway was hurrying and everyone was untidy, so no one paid the slightest attention to the ragged trio as they ran in pursuit of Sholto.

They caught up with him quite quickly. He was crouching beside a tearful little girl, deftly replacing a bandage on her arm.

"Now, do not pull it off again, Daisy," Rye heard him say.

"It hurts," the child whimpered.

"Of course," Sholto agreed seriously. "But it is not the bandage that hurts you. It is the cut underneath. The bandage will stop the bleeding and keep the dirt out. It is your friend. See?"

He pulled a pencil from his pocket and drew two eyes and a smiling mouth on the edge of the bandage. The little girl blinked, and slowly her face broke into a wobbly grin.

"The roof fell down on us," she said, as if confiding a great secret. "But Mistress Fife said we mustn't cry. She said it was good the roof was on us, because it kept us safe from the skimmers."

"Well, Mistress Fife was quite right," Sholto said lightly, rising to his feet. "I must go now, Daisy. Just remember — you take care of your friend, and your friend will take care of you."

The child nodded and began crooning to the face on the bandage. As he turned away, Sholto caught sight of Rye, Dirk, and Sonia and realized they had been watching him. He flushed slightly and stalked on down the hallway without a word. Their hearts too full to speak, they hurried after him.

In moments, they had reached the center of the rescue mission. There they found the gaping doorway that was the source of the shouts and clatters. There they found exhausted Wall workers staggering out of dusty gloom with sobbing children in their arms. There they found Tallus the healer, covered in blood, tenderly but thoroughly examining each small patient before passing him or her on with a curt order.

And there they found Faene of Fleet, coolly strapping sprained limbs and stitching wounds at Tallus's command. And Annocki, her green robe torn to ribbons, bandaging and soothing as if she had been doing it all her life.

Sonia gave a choked cry and flew to Annocki's side. Dirk remained rooted to the spot, staring at Faene as if he did not dare to move in case she disappeared.

Faene felt his gaze, raised her head from her work, and saw him. Her face lit up as if a candle flame had suddenly flared behind her eyes. Her golden skin was muddy with weariness. Her glorious tawny hair was scraped back and bundled heedlessly into a net. But Rye thought she had never looked so beautiful.

For an instant, it seemed that time had stood still. Then Faene bent her radiant face over her patient again, and Dirk threw back his shoulders, strode into the dimness beyond the Orphans' Door, and vanished.

"Faene could not sleep," Rye heard Annocki tell Sonia in a low voice. "She was awake when the attack came. She pulled me from my bed, actually dragged me to the door! I thought she was mad, but then we heard the tower crack. We escaped just before it fell."

"Ah!" cried Tallus, catching sight of Sholto. "So

you are back, my boy! Excellent! There are two broken arms, a broken leg and an ankle over there, waiting to be set. See to them, will you?"

It was as if he had seen his apprentice only yesterday.

"Tallus," Sholto began. "We —"

"Not now!" Tallus muttered, closing his eyes as he ran his fingers over the head of the unconscious child in front of him. "See to the patients. That young woman has a good, steady hand. She can assist you." He jerked his head at Annocki. Clearly he did not have the faintest idea who she was.

Sholto raised an eyebrow, but silently moved away to do the old healer's bidding. Annocki pushed a roll of bandages into Sonia's hands, gathered the tatters of her robe around her, and followed, very straight-backed. Sonia eyed the bandages helplessly, gnawing at her lip.

"Well, get on with it, girl!" Tallus snapped at her as another small patient was put down in front of him.

His sharp gaze fell on Rye, and he gave a little start. "Why, it is you, young Rye! What have you done to your hair? Your mother is here somewhere — ah, yes, I remember now, she is in the kitchen, brewing more remedies. Make some new bandages, will you? The pile of clean sheets is right beside you."

In the end, it was Sonia who tore the sheets into strips and Rye who took Annocki's place beside Faene, bandaging wounds. At first, he was as nervous and clumsy as Sonia had been when she tried the job, but gradually, with Faene's help, he became more confident.

"It is only a matter of practice," Faene said when he mumbled yet another apology for failing to keep up with her. But she glanced at him curiously all the same. She clearly found it very odd that a grown person would not know how to bandage a serious wound.

Rye reminded himself that for all her gentleness Faene had grown up not in the careful, protected world of Weld but in the rough-and-ready land beyond the Wall. Where she came from, children ran free, bloodhogs roamed, laws were few, and accidents and injuries were part of life. To Faene of Fleet, basic first aid was an ordinary life skill, like being able to ride a horse, make a fire, or patch a torn garment.

They worked feverishly as Wall workers, Dirk among them, brought a steady stream of new patients from above. But slowly the flow dwindled, and at last, the Keep healer limped through the door, leaning heavily on Dirk's arm. The healer had lost one of her shoes. Her bare foot, roughly bound with a filthy stocking, was hugely swollen. Her plump cheeks sagged with exhaustion and there was a great purple bruise on her forehead.

"There are no more," she said to Tallus. "The men are sealing the attics now. How is Fife — the nursemaid with the injured spine? I did my best to —"

"She is well enough," Tallus said gruffly. "What have you done to your foot, Linna?"

The woman looked down vaguely and shrugged. "Something fell on it. I had to cut the shoe away so I could go on working. I will see to it presently."

Tallus shook his head. "No, Linna, you will sit down right now and —" He broke off and squinted down the hallway. There was some sort of flurry there. The crowd was parting to let a hurrying figure pass.

Rye recognized the woman, Bettina. Most of the curling rags had come loose from her hair, but some still clung to her scalp like frayed moths. Her eyes were bright with excitement.

"Healer Tallus!" she panted as she drew closer. "Come quickly! The Warden is in the drawing room, and he is in a temper the like of which you have never seen! He wants everything put back the way it was. And when the others told him no, it was your orders that the sickest orphans be put to bed in the drawing room, he started flapping around a paper he says proves you are a traitor! Now he has called for soldiers to —"

Tallus gave a roar of rage. "See to the healer's foot!" he yelled at Faene. "I will be back!"

He set off along the hallway as fast as his limping gait would take him. Dirk, Sholto, Rye, and Sonia glanced at one another and followed.

"How can the Warden call you a traitor, Tallus?" Sholto demanded as soon as he reached the old healer's side. "Surely even he cannot think it is treason to move the furniture in his cursed drawing room?"

"Oh, he is probably talking about this," Tallus

said, pulling a crumpled paper from his pocket and pushing it into his apprentice's hands. "A little newsletter we started. First edition rushed out yesterday. The Wall workers are passing copies all around Weld."

Sholto groaned softly.

"What are you moaning about?" snapped Tallus, turning to glare at him. "We had to do something to make the fool see reason!"

He began crossing to the drawing-room side of the hallway, slowing only to step between the children lying in the center.

Rye craned to see the paper and managed to read the top of the page.

THE LANTERN

SOUTHWALL TO TEST NEW SKIMMER DEFENSE

The brave people of Southwall have volunteered to test, in their own streets, their healer Tallus's theory that we can repel the skimmers by flooding the night sky with light. They have sent a petition to the Warden asking for the Keep's assistance.

"All citizens of Weld should join the brave people of Southwall in urging the Warden to supply the large lanterns needed for our test," Healer Tallus told the *Lantern* as he left to deliver the petition. "The Warden must be made to face facts. The skimmer attacks are getting worse. Our old defenses are no longer good enough. If Weld is to survive, new ideas must be tested. If they fail, they fail. But they must be tried."

The full text of the petition, which was signed by every citizen of Southwall, is given overleaf.

"The Warden was in the middle of writing to forbid the test when the attack came," Sholto was telling Tallus by the time Rye had finished reading. "We saw the letter in the waiting room."

"I expected no less," Tallus panted. "Still, with luck, the *Lantern* will rouse enough anger in Weld for him to change his tune in time for the second test. We can get along without the Keep lanterns for the first if we must. Smaller lanterns in large numbers will do."

"Tallus," Sholto began, "I must tell you —"

But the old healer was no longer listening. They had reached the drawing room, and he was burrowing through the small crowd that had gathered outside the open doorway.

"*You!*" Rye heard the Warden bellow. "By the Wall, how do you dare show your face after what you have —?"

"Keep your voice down!" Tallus hissed. "There are sick children in here, in case you have not noticed. And there is to be no more talk about turning them out, Warden. You move them at your peril!"

TIME TO CHOOSE

Murmuring apologies in the polite Weld manner that Dirk and Sholto, at least, had almost forgotten, the companions edged to the front of the crowd at the doorway. The drawing room was filled with rows of stretchers on which children lay sleeping. Here and there a woman sat on the floor, holding the stretchers on either side of her as if to anchor them in place.

Tallus had stopped by the first row of stretchers. Facing him at a safe distance was the Warden, his face scarlet, his plump fingers clutching a sodden copy of the Southwall newsletter. The bald officer, Jordan, was standing by.

"Do not threaten me, Tallus!" the Warden was spluttering. "These foolish women do not know what you are, but I do!" He shook the wet paper at Tallus so violently that it tore. "You are behind this rag! Do not try to deny it! You are a — a traitor to Weld!"

The people in the doorway gasped. With a sinking feeling, Rye found the armor shell and pushed it onto his finger.

"A traitor, Warden?" Tallus said, his voice sharp with contempt. "Because I wanted to spread the word that there might be a chance of beating the skimmers? Because I wanted to make sure that if you tried to stop our test the whole of Weld would know? Well, put me in a cell if you like. It will make no difference."

The Warden's eyes bulged. He glanced at Jordan for help, but Jordan was staring stolidly ahead, and appeared not to notice.

"The Southwall test will go on, with me or without me," Tallus said, limping rapidly forward until he and the Warden were almost nose to nose. "The columns to raise the lanterns above roof level are being built as we speak. And if you attempt to have those columns pulled down, Warden, everyone will hear about it. The *Lantern* will see to that!"

"The *Lantern* will be suppressed!" the Warden squeaked. "We have discovered who is writing it, and he will be dealt with! What is the fellow's name, Jordan? Crane . . . Cren . . . ?"

"Crell, sir," Jordan said tonelessly.

Crell! Dirk's friend Crell! Rye felt a jolt in the pit of his stomach, and Dirk and Sholto became very still.

"It is hardly difficult to find out the name of the *Lantern's* editor," Tallus murmured. "It is printed at the bottom of the second page — quite plainly."

Some of the people in the doorway laughed. The Warden looked up sharply, as if noticing the crowd for the first time. Rye held his breath, but the watery eyes slid over the three brothers without showing a spark of recognition.

It would be a different story if I still had red hair, Rye thought, and shook his head. How strange that the disguise meant to hide him from enemies beyond the silver Door had been of the most use to him in Weld!

"We know of this Crell, as it happens," the Warden said loudly, his gaze still on the crowd. "Our records show that he came to the Keep years ago, claiming to be a quest volunteer. When it came to the point, however, he showed his true colors. He abandoned his brave comrades and crept home."

Jordan looked down his nose and smoothed his huge mustache. The people at the door fell silent.

"I daresay if he had not run away he would have been declared dead like all the others," said Tallus calmly. "And that would have been a pity, for me and for the whole of Weld. There are more ways than one to be a hero."

"A hero, indeed!" jeered the Warden. "We will see how brave he is when he is brought in under guard tomorrow!"

"Under guard for telling the truth?" a woman shrilled from the doorway. "Shame!"

Tallus smiled. "Oh, I doubt you will catch Crell, Warden," he said. "He and his printing device are very well hidden."

The crowd cheered.

"Jordan, shut that door!" the Warden roared.

A small boy woke and began to wail. The old woman with the braid rose from the floor and hurried to comfort him, shooting the Warden a furious glance.

"It might not be wise, sir, to let the citizens feel you have something to hide," Jordan said in a voice so low that Rye could scarcely hear it.

"Do as I say!" the Warden bellowed.

Two more children began to cry. Expressionless, Jordan moved to do as he was told.

"We will have to go in," Dirk muttered. "We cannot let Tallus face this alone. Rye, put on the armor . . ." His voice trailed off as Rye showed him the shell already clinging to his little finger.

Together the brothers darted into the room. Rye had the feeling that Sonia had moved at the same time, but he did not dare look around to be sure. He did not want to draw attention to her. What the Warden would say if he saw his daughter's maid in the company of rebels did not bear thinking about.

Jordan's attention, at least, was all for Dirk, Rye, and Sholto. He lunged for them, bounced back, and fell heavily to the floor. Shocked titters rippled through the crowd in the doorway. Gaping at the brothers, Jordan picked himself up and sidled to the door. It closed with a click, shutting the laughter out.

Dirk, Rye, and Sholto ranged themselves behind Tallus. The Warden stepped back, crossing his fingers and wrists as if to ward off evil.

"So you have brought your henchmen with you, Tallus!" he cried as Jordan returned to his side. "Now we know what you are, without doubt! Where are the soldiers, Jordan? What is the meaning of this delay?"

"You ordered that the men present themselves in clean uniforms, sir," said Jordan. "They had to change, but I am sure they will be here soon."

Sholto snorted. Dirk shook his head in disgust. Jordan eyed them keenly, then turned to gaze in puzzlement at Rye.

Jordan knows he has seen us before! Rye thought. In a moment, he will realize we were all quest volunteers. He will realize we have come from beyond the Wall.

"Hold them, Jordan!" the Warden ordered feverishly, pointing to Dirk, Rye, and Sholto. "Hold them here till I return! There is — something I have to do. In private!"

He turned and bolted into the waiting room, slamming the door behind him.

"He has probably gone to destroy the petition so he can pretend he never received it," Tallus murmured to Sholto out of the corner of his mouth. "You and your brothers had better make yourselves scarce, my boy, or you will find yourselves in a cell with me. Get back outside the Wall and keep trying to find the source of the skimmers. I cannot think why you have not done it by now — you have been away long enough!"

"We *have* found it!" Sholto snapped. "I have not had a chance to tell you."

"What?" Tallus thrust his hands through his hair and tugged at it violently. "But —"

"Listen, Tallus!" Sholto hissed. "There *is* an enemy, and he is breeding skimmers that can hunt in daylight."

"Daylight!" Tallus seemed to shrink.

"Yes. We destroyed most of the new breed, so your plan to light the darkness is good for now. It will save many lives. But in years to come —"

Tallus's eyes were wild. "Tell me — no! There is no time! Now it is more important than ever that you stay free. Go, my boy! Go while you can! I will see to it that your mother knows you are alive, never fear!"

Jordan was still staring at Dirk, Rye, and Sholto. He took a breath as if he was about to say something, but before he could speak, the hallway door opened and a group of very clean Keep soldiers marched in.

"Too late!" Tallus groaned. "Here are the stalker birds!"

Despite everything, Rye had to smile. The soldiers, with their red leggings, white tunics, and plumed helmets, did look ridiculously like the long-legged birds that plagued Weld's grain fields. Then the smile froze on his lips as another image flew into his mind — the image of inhuman, gray-uniformed guards with strangely smooth, cool skin, and hard, flat eyes.

How would the elegant Keep soldiers fare against the forces of the Lord of Shadows? The idea would have been comical if it had not been so terrible. It would not be battle, but slaughter.

But even as Rye shivered, it came to him abruptly that it did not really matter if Weld's defenders were strong or weak. No army, however used to fighting, could combat the Enemy's dark sorcery.

Instinctively he reached up to the little bag hanging around his neck. His fingers tingled with magic.

The waiting room door clicked open once more, and the Warden stood framed in the doorway. He had put on his plumed hat, despite the fact that the feathers were stained with ink. He strutted forward, not troubling to close the door behind him. Through the gap, Rye could see that the petition and the half-finished letter no longer lay on the polished table.

What am I doing here? Rye thought suddenly. *How could I have let myself be drawn back into the affairs of Weld when outside the Wall right now something may be happening that will take us all another step toward disaster? When I am the only one with magic enough to stop it?*

A feeling of urgency was surging within him like cold, salty water.

Sonia! he called in his mind.

The answer came instantly. *I am here — hidden behind the chairs piled at the Warden's back.*

Sonia, I must go back through the Wall, Rye thought frantically. *I must go — now!*

The answer rang in his mind like a crystal bell. *Make your move when you can. I will be with you.*

No argument. No questions. Yet Sonia had to know as well as Rye did that it would be a miracle if she, with no armor shell or speed ring to aid her, and no hood to conceal her, could reach him in time to share in his escape.

Dull pain stabbed in Rye's chest. He could not imagine going beyond the Wall without Sonia. What was more, his every instinct told him that it was wrong to leave her behind — that he needed her.

Roughly he forced his misery aside. If leaving Weld without delay meant leaving without Sonia, then that was how it had to be.

He took stock of his surroundings. The Warden had moved to Jordan's side once more. The soldiers stood rigidly to attention, spaced out in a ragged line among the small patients' beds. The waiting room door gaped wide not far to Rye's left.

It was almost too easy.

"This healer and his henchmen are traitors to Weld," the Warden was telling the soldiers. "When I give the order, move forward and take them into custody. Lock them up, then return at once to your duties. We must have the courtyard cleared in time for the changing of the guard."

"The — the changing of the guard, sir?" one of the soldiers stammered. "Today, sir?"

"Certainly," said the Warden with a slight frown.

The soldiers gaped at him, shifting uneasily from foot to foot so that they looked more like stalker birds than ever.

Rye gripped his brothers' arms. "Into the waiting room," he breathed. "Now!"

He moved, and his brothers moved with him. Sped by the enchanted ring, they were standing by the narrow door that led to the depths of the Keep while the Warden and his men were still yelling in shock. The golden key was ready in Rye's hand, but he did not need it. The padlock hung open, and the door stood slightly ajar.

"I fastened that padlock after we came through!" Sholto panted as he and Rye bolted into the stone stairway after Dirk. "I am sure of it!"

"Perhaps it opened when it felt our need of it," said a voice at Rye's back.

Rye spun around. Sonia was standing there, closing the door behind her. She was pale and breathless, but she was with him, just as she had promised. He stared at her, dazed with relief.

"Sonia!" Dirk exploded. "How did you get here?"

Sonia shrugged. "I ran when you did, that is all. Did you think you were rid of me, Dirk? It is not so easy."

Sholto was already hurrying down the steps. "Come on!" he urged. "Any moment they may realize where we have gone!"

Dirk, Rye, and Sonia followed him, their ears straining for the sound of heavy feet pounding after them. But all was still quiet as they reached the tiny jewel-like room at the bottom of the steps.

"They must have thought we escaped through the other waiting room door — the one we were all brought through to sign our Volunteer Statements," Dirk said gleefully.

Sonia had moved quickly to the golden medallion fixed to the wall opposite the door. Her dyed hair hung limply around her shoulders, and there were dark patches beneath her eyes. But the eyes were glittering green.

She is filled with excitement because she is about to leave Weld again, Rye thought as he, Dirk, and Sholto ran to her side. *The land beyond is calling her. Now that she knows Annocki is safe, she cannot wait!*

Sonia raised her hand and pressed her palm to the golden disc that the Warden called the Sign of Dann. And in a blink, they were back in the Chamber of the Doors.

They picked their way through the rubble to the far wall of the Chamber where the three Doors glimmered.

Magnificent gold. Mysterious silver. Sturdy wood bound with brass. And above them, the rhyme carved into the stone:

> **THREE MAGIC DOORS YOU HERE BEHOLD**
> **TIME TO CHOOSE: WOOD? SILVER? GOLD?**
> **LISTEN TO YOUR INNER VOICE**
> **AND YOU WILL MAKE THE WISEST CHOICE.**

Rye stared at the rhyme.

Time to choose . . .

The three words seemed to loom at him from the rock, larger than all the rest, as if they were demanding his special attention.

Rye had opened a Door twice before, but in both cases, he had chosen with his mind, not with his heart. Now, at last, he was free to do what the rhyme told him to do. He could choose for himself. And now that the moment had come, he was afraid.

He tore his eyes from the carving and glanced to his left, where his brothers stood in silence. Dirk was staring longingly at the golden Door. Sholto's eyes were fixed on the silver. Rye could read their thoughts as clearly as if they had been spoken aloud.

Dirk was thinking that behind the golden Door he would find strong allies, plentiful supplies, horses, and weapons to combat the Enemy. After rescuing so many injured children, he was thirsting for revenge and longing for the chance to fight.

Sholto was brooding on his failure to find and destroy the skimmers that were being sent to ravage Weld. He was thinking that behind the silver Door lay the Enemy's stronghold, where surely those skimmers must be. He wanted the chance to finish what he had begun.

And both brothers were bitterly regretting their promise to follow Rye through the wooden Door that for some reason had taken his fancy, but which led into the unknown.

Then Rye looked to his right, at Sonia. She was staring straight ahead. Rye followed her gaze and was transfixed. He gazed at the sturdy old timber and mellow brass of the third Door, and a great longing rose in him, overwhelming his doubts.

Time to choose . . .

Sonia drew him close, and together they stepped toward the wooden Door. Dirk and Sholto moved with them. Rye was glad of it but knew that even if his brothers had given way to their regrets he would not have faltered.

Sonia raised her hand, then glanced at him. Rye nodded. She had waited even longer than he had for this.

Sonia grasped the heavy ring that served as a handle for the wooden Door. She twisted the ring. She pulled. And the Door swung smoothly open, beckoning them in.

VOICES

No unseen force dragged Rye through the third Door as it had when the other two Doors opened for him. This time, his own feet carried him forward, and it was only when the wooden Door swung silently shut behind them that he realized it had led them into the dark.

He stood rigid in echoing dimness. He could hear the hollow gurgle of running water. He breathed in musty air tainted with the faint, sweet reek of death. He heard Sonia draw a sharp breath, heard Dirk mutter a curse, felt Sholto's hand tighten on his shoulder. The blood was pounding in his ears. What was this place that felt and smelled like a tomb?

His stomach tightened as he realized that his urge to go through the third Door had been so strong that it had driven everything else from his mind. He had forgotten to pull the hood of concealment over his head. He had forgotten to check that the armor shell was still fastened to his little finger. He had forgotten to make sure that the bag of charms was safe around his neck, and that he had not lost the bell tree stick.

Even as his hand flew to his belt he thought it strange that he was checking the least important thing first. What would it matter if the stick was lost? As a weapon it was next to useless. Yet exquisite relief flooded through him as he found the stick was still with him, smooth, sturdy, and familiar. He gripped it, feeling his mind steady and his breathing slow.

His eyes were adjusting, too. It was not quite as dark as he had first thought. He could make out the shapes of his companions. He could see the dense shadow of rock on either side of them. He could see that the wall ahead was lighter than the rest.

He dipped his fingers into the brown bag. As he touched the light crystal, the bag lit up like a lantern, and even before he had drawn the crystal out his companions were sighing in relief.

They were not in a tomb but in a narrow cave, its mouth masked by a thick curtain of vine.

Dirk reached the vine curtain in three strides and began tearing it away. Sonia and Rye were close behind him.

"Take care!" Sholto warned.

But already there was a large hole in the barrier, and as far as Rye could see, nothing was lurking on the other side.

The vine was thick and its stems were tough, but soon its ruins lay in a heap on the floor of the cave, and the four companions were stumbling into a magical world of soft light and damp, tangy air.

Gigantic trees rose before them. Rain-wet vine studded with purple flowers clothed the mighty trunks and hung in great swags from the trees' lower branches. Running water sang and gurgled on every side. Mist rose from the forest floor and drifted up to the dripping green canopy that hid the sky.

"The Fell Zone," Sonia whispered.

Rye looked quickly around. Rain-spangled spiderwebs sparkled here and there, but there were none of the sagging, stringy nets of the fell-dragons. It was deliciously cool compared to the stuffiness of the cave and the stale warmth of the Keep. The flowery vine veils, gleaming with damp and wreathed in mist, were beautiful. But the odor of death still drifted in the air, and no birds sang.

"I remember this," Sholto said quietly. "In the part where I was it was very dim because great mats of vine stretched from tree to tree, blocking all the light from above. But I remember vast trunks like these, caves like the one behind us, giant rocks, some hollow and some solid. And — yes!"

He spun around.

Rye turned to see what he was looking at. Behind them, rock sloped steeply upward, striped with twisting rivulets of water, and dotted here and there with bushes and trees. The cave gaped at its base, still thickly fringed with vine.

"I formed the theory that Weld was actually inside a hollow mountaintop — inside the crater of a dead volcano!" Sholto exclaimed. "I remember writing about it! Ah, if only my notebook had not been destroyed!"

He was speaking much faster than usual. There was warm color in his face and a light in his eyes that Rye had not seen for a very long time.

"If I am right, the Wall began as a simple shell of natural rock," Sholto went on, striding back to the cave and squatting to examine it. "The first settlers began coating the rock with bricks on the inside — to seal holes and cracks at first, no doubt, then to strengthen thin patches, and then — well, if our Warden's ancestors were anything like him, perhaps just to make Weld look tidy!"

Dirk was shaking his head in amazement, but Rye was finding it harder and harder to concentrate. Something had begun pushing at the edges of his mind. A feeling of dread was growing within him. He found that he had crossed his fingers and his wrists and slowly uncrossed them. Simple charms would not protect him here.

The bag of powers hanging around his neck seemed to warm against his skin. He gripped it and fought the dread down.

"This *must* be the Fell Zone, Rye," Sonia said in a

low voice. "It can be nothing else! But it is so different from the part we saw beyond the golden Door!"

Dirk shrugged. "The Fell Zone fills the whole of Dorne's center, Sonia. It is so deep that Weld has been hidden in its heart for a thousand years. You cannot expect it all to look the same."

"But this place does not just *look* different," Sonia said, biting her lip. "It *feels* different. It feels . . . angry."

Rye shivered. Sonia was right. The rage in the forest was like a living thing.

And then the whispering began, hissing in his ears, mingling with the sound of dripping leaves and running water.

Leave this place, Rye of Weld!

Fellan! There were Fellan here, watching and listening. They were the source of the anger that was weighing him down.

The nine powers are of no use to you here. Go!

The hissing voices were strange to him. These watchers were not the Fellan who had given him the bag of powers. But they knew of him — knew his name! And it seemed to Rye that their anger could mean only one thing. These Fellan must have learned or sensed that he had caused the tyrant Olt's death and opened the way to the Lord of Shadows.

Begone, Rye of Weld!

Sweat sprang out on Rye's forehead. "We are not wanted here," he heard himself say, and he saw Sonia nod.

Dirk looked at them keenly. Once he might have scoffed and told them to stop imagining things. He knew better now.

"Then we had better leave while we can," he said grimly. "We —" He broke off, staring at Sholto.

Sholto was crouched at one side of the cave entrance, carefully pushing loops of vine aside with a thick strip of bark. He had found the source of the smell. Entangled in the vine was the dead body of a skimmer.

"I remember this!" Sholto said, glancing up at his companions before turning his attention back to his grisly find. "I remember finding dead skimmers. I remember examining them!"

He prodded one of the skimmer's wings, which was twisted and broken, then uncovered the head.

"Pale eyes," he said with a sigh of relief. "Not one of the Master's new breed, then. No doubt this specimen had stayed out too long and was blinded by the sun. It crashed against the rock face, slid down, and was entangled in the vine."

Go! Go! Leave our place!

The whispering in Rye's mind was so loud now that he felt his head must burst. He had begun to shiver. His legs ached with the urge to run.

"Perhaps it is from this part of Dorne, not from the Harbor, that the beasts are being sent to Weld!" he heard Sonia exclaim. "Perhaps the Master has another stronghold somewhere here! That would explain last night's attack."

"I have been thinking the same thing," Sholto agreed. "The workers at the Harbor are not aware that any other base exists, but they are isolated and know only what they are told."

"Then what are we waiting for?" Dirk snapped. "If there is another base, let us get out of these cursed trees and find it!"

With shaking hands, Rye pulled the hood over his head. As his companions gathered around him and he took the feather from the brown bag, the voices in his mind swelled to a triumphant clamor. He gritted his teeth and tried to ignore them. He told himself that the Fellan had not won. They were not driving him away. He was leaving the Fell Zone because he wished to.

But as he rose with his companions through the misty air, and the whispers slowly faded from his mind, the relief was so intense that he felt dizzy. Only then did he admit to himself how much his resistance to the Fellan had cost him. Only then did he wonder if he could have stood against their will for much longer.

And only then did he wonder, with a prickle of fear, what would have happened if the Fellan had lost patience and decided to rid their forest of the unwelcome visitors by doing more than simply sending them away.

Before the companions reached the treetops, the sun came out, transforming the mist into a shining golden haze. It became very difficult to see anything at all, but once they were above the muffling trees, they did not need their sight to tell them which way to go. They could hear sounds coming from below, not very far away.

Music. Singing. The roar of voices. The occasional whinny of a horse. There were people, many people, somewhere near.

"Our search will not be long, it seems," Dirk muttered. "Who else but the Master would place a settlement so close to the Fell Zone?"

"I never heard music played at the Harbor," Sholto said dubiously.

Dirk grimaced. "They are celebrating the attack on the Keep last night, perhaps."

Rye turned toward the sound, and as he and his companions began to glide rapidly through the shining mist, he felt a small stab of triumph. The Fellan below might resent his possession of the bag of powers, but they could not stop him from using it. He had found it very hard to control the power of the feather at first. Now he had mastered it, as he had learned to master all the other powers at his command.

No, he thought suddenly. *Not all. The sweet that smells of honey is still a mystery. And I still do not know what the ninth power is — or even if there is a ninth power! For all I know, the ninth power was lost or stolen from the bag long ago.*

"Rye!" Sonia's warning whisper jolted Rye out of his thoughts. He realized that he had lost height. His feet were brushing the topmost leaves of the trees. He put the Fellan and the powers out of his mind, focused again on the sounds ahead, and sped on.

"Curse this mist!" Dirk complained, leaning dangerously forward and peering down. "I cannot see a thing!"

But in a very few minutes, the companions had reached the end of the trees, and as they flew lower, they began to catch glimpses of the bushes and rocks that marked the forest's fringe.

Then, abruptly, a tall, dark barrier was looming out of the mist in front of them. With Sonia's cry of alarm ringing in his mind and his brothers' yells loud in his ears, Rye managed to soar steeply upward just in time to skim over what seemed to be a fence made of great sheets of metal.

How he had done it he did not know. In another moment, they would have crashed into the barrier as fatally as a sun-blinded skimmer slamming into a rock face. His heart thudding wildly at the narrow escape, Rye took a moment to realize that the voices and music had suddenly become very much louder.

"By the Wall, look at that!" he heard Dirk breathe, and at last glanced down.

Beyond the fence there was a small lake bobbing with ducks. From the lake, a narrow river confined between banks of stone flowed peacefully between clumps of trees. A paved road kept company with the river, and beside the road, a huge pipeline was being built, its bulky stone supports marching all the way to the distant hills.

But close, very close, just where the river began, sprawled a rough, untidy town that throbbed with life.

People in bright, festive clothes thronged the town's muddy streets, which were lined with very simple stone and metal dwellings. In the large central square, more people sat at long tables beneath striped awnings, eating, drinking, singing, and pounding the tabletops in time to the rollicking tune being played by a nearby band of fiddlers. Others were dancing, stamping on the bare ground, careless of the mud the rain had left behind. Stalls choked the narrow side streets. Everywhere there were peddlers shouting their wares while busily selling sugared apples on sticks, dolls, jewelry, and embroidered shawls to eager customers.

The people were of every kind, every color, every size and shape. There were small people like the tribe from Nanny's Pride farm and like FitzFee, who had saved Rye from a bloodhog beyond the golden Door. There were tall people like the fishing folk of Oltan and the scourers of the Den. A few soldiers in blue uniforms mingled with the crowd, but there were no gray guards, no slave hunters — no sign of the Master at all.

Invisible beneath the protection of Rye's hood, the companions landed beside the river amid a clutter of upturned canoes. Behind the barrier fence, the Fell

Zone trees rose high, dark and secret, concealing the rocky summit where the companions had begun their flight.

"Where in Weld are we?" Dirk whispered.

Sonia pointed to a banner that had been strung between two trees facing a sturdy wooden jetty.

WELCOME TO FELL END, CHIEFTAIN FARR!

"Fell End?" Dirk shook his head in puzzlement. "I have never heard of it! In Fleet and Oltan, I was told there were no other towns in Dorne — except for the exiles' camp in the east. Who are these people?"

Sholto raised an eyebrow. "And who, I wonder, is Chieftain Farr?"

"I think," said Rye, staring downriver, "we are about to find that out."

FELL END

An odd-looking vessel had come into view from behind a clump of trees, pushing along the ribbon of water with a faint chugging sound. It was square and low, with a steaming funnel. Many small red-and-yellow flags fluttered gaily above the heads of several figures gathered on its deck. As Sonia, Sholto, and Dirk turned to look, a great cloud of steam billowed from the boat's funnel, and there was a long, loud hoot.

Yells of excitement rose from the town. The music stopped, and people began swarming toward the little jetty.

By the time the strange craft arrived, a small knot of self-conscious men and women had gathered beneath the banner to greet the visitors. Behind them, the mud-spattered townspeople were chattering, waving, and cheering lustily.

As the vessel was tied securely, Rye wondered which of its passengers was Chieftain Farr. Was it the man with the lean face and sunken eyes in a long black robe and a close-fitting black cap? Was it the haughty woman with the coronet of iron-gray braids and the very correct dark green gown that covered her from wrist to ankle?

Was it the plump old woman who looked like a kind grandmother in a book of fairy tales? Or the elegant, golden-skinned woman smiling beside her? Or could Farr possibly be the beefy, red-faced man in a blue velvet coat and frilled shirt who was furtively tugging at his high collar as if it was strangling him?

As the gangplank slid into place, Rye discovered that it was none of them. The crowd roared as a big, black-haired man rose to tower above his companions, holding the small boy he had stooped to pick up in one arm. The man gave his free arm to the elegant woman, and they moved over the gangplank together.

"Farr!" the crowd chanted. "Farr! Farr! Farr!"

The big man grinned, then put the little boy down and stepped forward to shake hands with the officials on the jetty. His boots shone and his white shirt was spotless, but these were the only things that set him apart from the people who greeted him so eagerly. His thick hair was already springing back into an untidy bush, despite the water that had been used to smooth it down. His hands were brown and rough, with strong, blunt fingers. He looked a little like Hass, the fisherman who had helped Rye in Oltan. Perhaps that was why Rye liked and trusted him on sight.

Farr introduced his companions to the crowd simply and without ceremony.

The hollow-eyed man, it seemed, was called Manx, and was a member of what Farr called his advisory council. The woman with the braids, Sigrid of Gold Marsh, was also a council member, and so was the stout man, whose name was Barron.

The crowd clapped politely when the first two were named, and with more energy as Barron made his clumsy bow. But when Farr presented his wife, Janna, his son, Zak, and the sweet-faced old woman who was Zak's nurse, Petronelle, there was a roar of cheers.

"They care more for their chieftain's family than for the council members, it seems," Sholto muttered.

"They are moved because Farr has brought his wife and son with him," said Dirk. "Living hard by the Fell Zone, these people must face danger every day. Farr is showing them that he and his family are willing to share that danger, and they love him for it."

Sholto raised an eyebrow. Rye was smiling to himself, thinking that for all Sholto's cleverness, he would never understand people as Dirk did, when he felt a cold shadow slide into his mind.

Hatred. Malice. Danger . . .

A terrible feeling of foreboding, even worse than the dread he had felt in the Fell Zone, gripped Rye's heart. He sensed nothing from Sonia, but when he turned to her he realized why. She was curled up in the shadow of a canoe, fast asleep.

In confusion, he turned back to face the jetty. Farr was speaking again.

"I can see by your banner, friends, that you've remembered what I told you at the beginning of your great task, far from here and three long years ago," Farr said, looking out at the sea of eager faces. "I'm glad of it. The future's in your hands now, as your work nears its end, just as truly as it was then. By your sweat, blood, and courage, thousands of people who might never know your names will live and prosper. On their behalf, I offer you my deepest thanks."

He waited for the wild applause to die down before going on.

"When I stood for election as your chieftain, I said that I respected our traditions and would resist change for change's sake. I promised to be cautious. But I also swore that if the slay attacks and other acts of violence didn't stop, I'd take action."

Thunderous cheers. Rye, Dirk, and Sholto looked at one another in shock.

"Slay attacks!" hissed Dirk. "By the Wall —"

Farr held up his hands to silence the cheers.

"In less than a week, I'm told, the pipeline you've built will reach Fell End," he said. "As you know, it's a key part of our plan —"

"But how, Farr?" someone shouted from the back of the crowd. "Won't you tell us even now?"

The officials on the jetty looked embarrassed by the interruption. Farr only grinned. "I know how curious you must be, friend," he called. "But the secret has to be kept for now. The enemy mustn't suspect our plan until everything's in place and we can bargain from a position of real strength."

"Why bargain?" a woman cried shrilly. "Fight, I say! Avenge our dead!"

Many in the crowd shouted agreement.

Farr's grin faded and he shook his head. "Revenge won't bring back the people we've lost," he said soberly. "It won't repair homes, or build up our herds and crops again. If we can stop the attacks by threats alone, I'll be more than satisfied."

There were few cheers this time. Clearly most in the crowd were disappointed. Behind Farr's back, the councilors Manx and Sigrid exchanged dubious glances. Barron, his plump red face puckered in concern, pulled out a handkerchief and mopped his sweating brow.

Farr squared his shoulders. "Peace is what I hope for, yes! I've never made any secret of that. But all who hear me now can be sure of one thing."

He had raised his voice slightly. His keen eyes searched the crowd.

He believes there are enemy spies here, Rye thought suddenly. *He is speaking to them as much as to these workers.*

"A wish for peace doesn't mean weakness," Farr went on, his face very stern. "If we have to attack to save ourselves, then attack we will. And our move will be swift, final, and delivered without mercy."

The crowd was his again. He stood for a moment, unsmiling, as the storm of cheers, stamps, and whistles broke over him. Then he offered his arm to his wife, and together they moved off the jetty with their son and the nurse, the three councilors, and the flustered welcoming party following.

"So, Rye," Dirk said tensely, "your instinct was right. The wooden Door has led us to an ally we did not know existed! Ten to one the pipeline is to supply water to troops in the Scour."

"That is all very fine," Sholto muttered as the crowd engulfed Farr and the band struck up again, "but Farr is dreaming if he thinks his threats will stop the Master. He plainly has no idea what he is dealing with!"

"None," Dirk agreed grimly. "We must get to him and warn him — tell him what we know."

"You two go," said Rye. "I will stay with Sonia."

"That is pointless, Rye," Dirk said impatiently. "Sonia is safe here, and she will not stir in the little time we will be away. When that girl decides she is tired, nothing can wake her! Remember how she was on the roof of the Harbor? Dead to the world, amid all that excitement! She is a mystery to me!"

"She is . . . remarkable," Sholto murmured.

Rye glanced at him sharply. Sholto was looking down at Sonia with a gentle, puzzled expression Rye had never seen on his face before.

So, Rye thought in confusion. *Sholto . . . Sonia . . .*

For some reason, he felt a pain in his heart.

"Throw back the hood, Rye," Dirk ordered. "We do not need it here, and in fact, it will hinder us. We need to be able to mingle with the crowd, talk to people while we wait for our chance to get Farr alone."

Rye looked around. The riverbank was deserted. There was no one to see them appear. Slowly he pushed back the hood and followed his brothers to the little jetty.

"I still cannot think how Nanion of Fleet, for example, had not heard of Farr and his settlement," Dirk said as they moved into the bustling main street of the town.

"Perhaps more people escaped from Olt's domain than Olt or anyone else knew," Rye suggested. "They could have slipped away in secret, a few at a time, many years ago."

As he spoke, they reached the town square, which was as big as a small field and seething with people. Farr and his wife were standing together in a small island of space in the center, admiring a pair of beautiful honey-colored horses being displayed by a small man who reminded Rye strongly of FitzFee. Nearer to the brothers, the long tables were being stocked with fresh platters of food, and the benches were filling.

Another banner flapped above the tables.

TO CELEBRATE CHIEFTAIN FARR'S VISIT, FREE FOOD AND DRINK TODAY!

"What luck!" Dirk exclaimed. "I am ravenous! We can eat and pick up some gossip at the same time."

As they squeezed onto the end of a bench, those farther along made room for them in friendly fashion. A plump, cheery woman sitting on the other side of the table pushed a metal platter toward them. The platter was heaped with wooden skewers threaded with grilled vegetables and chunks of meat.

"New around here, aren't you?" the woman asked as the brothers thanked her. "Heard there was work to be had, I daresay? Well, you heard true. A week will see the pipeline finished, but there'll still be plenty of cleaning up to do after that, and good hands are always welcome. Not everyone has the stomach to work out here. Tuck in!"

The food was wonderful. The meat was spicy and tender, like nothing Rye had ever tasted before. Juice ran down his chin, and he wiped it away with the back of his hand without a thought for Weld manners.

"Oh, very good!" Dirk mumbled with his mouth full.

"Just what I was saying," said the little man beside him. "They've done us proud today. Best bit of hog I've ever eaten."

Dirk and Rye froze, their cheeks bulging. Sholto carefully put his skewer down.

The woman laughed heartily. "They think you mean old-style bloodhog, Sol!" She leaned across the table and patted Dirk's hand. "It's the new breed, lovely," she explained kindly. "Descended from wild bloodhogs, they say, but bred and raised in Riverside. You'd have passed fields full of them on your way upriver — didn't you notice? No horns, no nasty tempers, and flesh as sweet as a hoji nut!"

Dirk nodded weakly. He swallowed what was in his mouth and quickly drained the beaker of ale that a sweating boy in a long, grubby apron had set down before him.

The joke of the strangers who thought they had eaten bloodhog spread around the table. Soon everyone was chortling and taunting the newcomers. Rye blushed and Sholto looked down his nose, but Dirk grinned broadly, lifted a fresh beaker of ale, and toasted his tormenters, earning himself a hearty cheer.

After that, Dirk and his brothers were treated as old friends. Food was pressed on them till they could eat no more. Their hopes of learning more about Farr, the pipeline, and Fell End proved fruitless, because so many people had begun singing along with the band that it was impossible to talk without roaring. But it was so good to sit with a full stomach in good company for a time that in truth they minded this very little.

I have not felt so at home since . . . since before Dirk and Sholto went away, Rye thought dreamily. At the same moment, he felt the armor shell freeing itself from his fingertip. It had sensed that he had relaxed. Quickly he caught it and stuffed it back into the brown bag, twisting a little aside so that no one would see.

As he turned back to the table, there was a stir. Chieftain Farr was leading his smiling lady into the circle of dancers. Benches quickly emptied as people jumped up to join the widening ring.

"Oh, imagine dancing with Farr!" cried the cheery woman, looking hopefully at Dirk. And in a moment, Dirk was on his feet, gallantly offering her his hand.

"You, too," he hissed at Sholto over his shoulder. "Talk as you dance! This is our chance to find a few things out at last!"

Dirk had not thought to ask Rye, and for this, Rye was profoundly grateful. He sat unnoticed on the end of the empty bench, smiling as Sholto bowed stiffly to a young woman with yellow bows in her hair and led her away with a sour look on his face. Sholto hated dancing.

Rye wondered how Sonia felt about it. He wondered if she had woken. He called her softly in his mind but received no reply.

Leave her be, he told himself. *You do not need Sonia at your elbow every moment.* He slid around on the bench, turning his back on the dancers.

The other side of the square was now almost deserted. The chieftain's son, Zak, was solemnly inspecting a solitary peddler's collection of brightly glazed pottery animals while his old nurse vanished into the little maze of stalls in a side street. As Rye watched, the boy suddenly made his choice and proudly handed a coin to the peddler.

His last sale made, the peddler closed his tray and departed. Zak was left alone. For a moment, he stood patiently waiting for his nurse to return, then his attention seemed to be attracted by something nearby. Rye squinted to see what the boy was looking at. At first, he could see nothing; then, suddenly, he caught a glimpse of something extraordinary.

A shining bubble was floating in midair, an arm's length from Zak's nose. The boy stretched out his hand, but the bubble moved a little away from him. He hesitated, then ran after it. The bubble drifted again, toward a shadowy doorway, and again the boy followed.

A creeping chill trickled down Rye's spine. Instinctively he rose, then realized that he should not approach the boy alone. However he felt about this place and its people, he was a stranger. He should not draw attention to himself. He looked around for help, looked back at Zak, and felt a surge of relief as he saw someone he recognized moving out of the darkness of the doorway.

Then sweat broke out on his forehead. As the familiar features emerged from the gloom, they were changing. They were melting, and re-forming. The skin was thickening, bulging and splitting till the head, limbs, and swollen body were shapeless masses of rough bark sprouting fat tongues of white fungus. The eyes were dark green holes. The hair was brightening, standing out from the head like crackling flames. Great, thorny claws were sprouting from the outstretched hands. And Zak screamed like a baby goat in peril as the shining bubble burst in his face and the monster leaped at him, claws reaching, wide jaws gaping like a trap.

Rye leaped at the same moment, with all the power of the speed ring behind him. His only weapon was the bell tree stick, but the stick was in his hand as he threw himself between the beast and the child.

Dimly he heard screams of alarm and the sounds of running feet. He thought he felt Sonia wake and cry out to him. He felt a great thud as the monster collided with him. He was blinded by a flash of white light. . . .

Then his head struck the ground, and there was only darkness.

THE STRANGER

Rippling. Chugging. The feeling of movement. A narrow bed. A blanket, soft beneath his fingers. Two voices murmuring, one low and husky, the other older and harsher. The smell of warm metal mingled with a faint lemony scent . . .

He struggled to remember what had happened to him, but memory would not come. His head ached. His mind was a maze of shadows. *Injured*, he thought. *I have been injured. But how . . . why?*

"Zak is with Farr on deck," the husky voice said. "Already he has almost recovered from his fright."

"It's all my fault," the harsher voice answered. "I'd never have left him, only he was taking so long to choose, and when that lying messenger came saying there was another buyer for that shawl I wanted, I . . ."

"Do not blame yourself, Petronelle," the husky voice whispered. "How could you have known it was a trick to lure you away at the right moment?"

"I *should* have known. I should have guessed —" The harsh old voice broke off in a sob.

"That is foolish talk!" the husky voice chided gently. "None of us thought that Zak was at risk in Fell End. Perhaps there was danger for Farr — he and I were prepared for that. But Zak — why Zak?"

There was a moment's silence. The boat chugged. It *was* a boat, the listener in the bed knew. He did not know what had happened to him. He did not even know his own name. But somehow he knew he was in a boat — and not on the sea, but on a river. A long, narrow river . . .

The chugging sound deepened. The boat was slowing, stopping.

"Riverside," the husky voice whispered. "Farr is leaving us here. I wish he was not, but it is necessary after what happened. He must be the one who tells the story or rumors will spread like wildfire."

"I don't understand why we aren't leaving the young stranger in Riverside with the other wounded," the harsh voice rasped. "While he is with us, Zak's memory of that horror will stay fresh. Better the child forgets."

"Zak is not so fragile, Petronelle. And Farr and I want to keep the stranger close. He risked his life to save our son. He deserves our every care."

"He'd get good care at Riverside. You can't fool me, Janna — I've known you too long. Farr wants the boy under his eye — you might as well admit it!"

There was a low, rueful laugh. "You are right, of course. Farr wants to question him when he has recovered. He may have seen something before the attack —"

"We all saw what happened, Janna! The beast spat white fire. It felled all who stood against it, and then it vanished. It was a thing of sorcery! You saw what it looked like! You know who sent it perfectly well!"

The beast . . .

Hideous images flashed into the mind of the listener in the bed. Hide like bark, hair like fire, craggy jaws gaping like a trap.

With the flashes came hot, pounding pain. He groaned.

There was a rustle of skirts. A soft hand touched his forehead. The lemony scent wafted over him.

"You are safe," he heard the husky voice say. "But your head is injured, so you must try to keep it still."

He felt a thudding jolt, heard rough shouts and the sound of wood squeaking on wood.

"Where . . . ?" His voice was a thin croak.

"You are in our barge. We are taking you downriver to where you can be cared for properly. Do not try to talk anymore. Rest now."

Noise outside. Chain rattling. Voices . . .

"Gently now . . . badly burned . . ."

". . . the worst of them with us. Another thirty or so still at Fell End."

". . . straight for young Zak! In another moment, he'd have been . . ."

". . . the last straw for Farr. Has to be."

The soft hand was taken away. The skirts rustled. The scent faded a little.

"I will ask for the shields to be lowered early. That will keep some of the noise out. Look after him, Petronelle. He is not to be left alone — not for a minute."

A door opened and closed. Someone sighed heavily, then moved to the bed and bent over him. There was no lemony fragrance this time, just a warm, soapy scent like clean sheets dried in the sun. He forced his heavy eyelids open. Mistily he saw a plump old face surrounded by a halo of fluffy white hair. A pair of sharp eyes, one green and one brown, looked keenly into his. The pursed mouth opened.

"You'll do," the mouth said.

There was a sliding, rasping sound, and the room darkened. The sounds from outside dulled.

"That's the shields coming down," the mouth said. "Time to sleep."

The stranger who had no name closed his eyes and slept.

❋

When he woke again, the room was pitch dark. He could still hear the soft chugging but now there were other sounds, too — muffled flapping, scrabbling sounds that for some reason filled him with dread.

He was not alone in the room. He could hear faint snores in the darkness. Dimly he remembered the old face that had peered down at him.

He could see nothing, but his other senses seemed abnormally sharp. He heard a tiny click. There was a slight movement in the air as if a door had opened and closed.

Evil had entered the room. He could feel it. He could hear it breathing. It slid toward him, full of hate. His head pounded. He tried to cry out but could not. He tried to move and could not. Evil was beside him. Evil loomed over him, cold and dreadful. He knew death was moments away.

The door swung wide open. A bright light bobbed through the doorway, and with the light tiptoed a small figure in a white nightshirt. The presence beside the bed stiffened and vanished into the shadows.

"Beware!" croaked the patient, finding his voice at last. He struggled to sit up, fell back with a groan, and felt the evil leave the room as swiftly as it had come.

"Petronelle!" the small figure cried in fright, the lantern swinging dangerously as he darted forward.

There was a snort from the other side of the room. An instant later, the old woman was at the bedside, smoothing her ruffled hair with one hand and feeling her patient's forehead with the other.

"What are you doing out of bed, Zak?" she

scolded, turning on the figure with the lantern. "And what do you mean by waking this poor fellow?"

"He was awake already, Petronelle!" the child protested. "And there was someone else here! Right beside him!"

"Nonsense!" snapped the old woman, snatching the lantern from him and holding it high. "There's no one here! You've been having nightmares, young man, that's what you've been having!"

"He must have gone out the door when I shouted," said Zak, blinking around.

"Nonsense!" Petronelle said again. She scowled down at her patient, handed the lantern back to Zak, and bustled away.

"She'll make you hot tea and honey now," Zak whispered, moving closer to the bed. "She always does that if I wake in the nighttime."

A brightening light on the other side of the room, and a series of little clanks and chinks showed that he was right. Above their heads, the scratching, flapping, brushing sounds went on.

"Danger," the patient managed to say.

His mind was still on the intruder, but Zak had already put that mystery out of his mind and was looking up at the ceiling.

"I know," he said, trying to sound matter-of-fact. "The enemy sends the slays to kill us when the sun goes down. Not where we live — only out here. But we're safe in the barge, Mother says, because of the slay

72

shields on the windows and because of the water. Slays hate water — did you know that?"

Slays. Water. Do I know . . . ?

The little boy looked down at him, waiting for an answer. When none came, his brow wrinkled.

"Zak!" Petronelle called softly. "Leave the stranger be! Get off back to bed and be quick about it before your mother finds you gone!"

Zak sighed. He turned toward the door, then suddenly swung back.

"I forgot," he whispered, and pushed something into the patient's hands. "This is yours. I kept it safe for you."

"*Zak!*" The old woman's voice was full of warning this time.

The child scuttled from the room, his swinging lantern sending crazy shadows leaping on the walls.

"Young scamp," Petronelle grumbled.

With difficulty, the patient lifted his hands and peered at the thing the child had given him. It was a stick — a smooth, sturdy stick.

Something emerged from the mists that clouded his mind. It was the image of a small tree covered in blossom and humming with bees. Not here. Somewhere else. Where?

He strained to sharpen the image, to remember. His head pounded.

"There," the woman said crossly at the bedside. "He's upset you. Take a little of this."

73

A spoon approached his lips. Sweet, warm liquid slipped down his throat. He took another spoonful, then another. The pain in his head eased.

"That's better." The harsh old voice seemed very far away. "What's this you've got? Oh, some rubbish of Zak's, is it? Here, let me . . ."

A hand plucked at the stick. He tightened his fingers around it.

"Keep it, then, if you want to, poor fellow," the old voice said. "Rest now. All's well."

Nothing is well, the stranger thought. He drifted back into sleep, holding the stick like a talisman.

❋

He woke again to dazzling sunlight, to painful jolting, to the dull crashing of waves, to the jingling of harness, the clopping of hooves, and the noise and smells of a city. Then somehow he was in a soft bed, between cool sheets in a dim, quiet room.

Dreamlike days and nights followed — days and nights of slipping in and out of sleep, of slowly ebbing pain, of firm but gentle hands tending him like a baby. Sometimes he dreamed that someone was calling him, but when he woke, he could never remember what the voice had said.

Gradually the room became familiar to him. He knew the window opposite where he lay, kept closed and shaded when the sun was strong, opened to let in a tangy sea breeze and a glimpse of sky at other times. He knew the cot behind the screen in the corner where

Petronelle dozed at night, and the little stove where she made the broth he drank from a cup with a spout. He knew the armchair by the window where Petronelle often sat sewing or knitting.

And he knew the wooden chair beside his bed. He always turned his head to it first when he stirred. Often it would be empty, but sometimes a golden-skinned woman would be there, smiling at him, the lemony scent of her perfume sweet in the air.

At last, however, there came a day when he woke completely — woke enough to realize he was wearing a clean white nightshirt and that a bandage was bound around his head. Woke enough to notice and examine curiously the little ring of plaited threads that he wore on his finger. Woke enough to wonder how long it had been since he stood on his feet, how long he had been in this room.

The window was open. He could see bright sky outside. He could hear the rattling of carts and the distant cries of seabirds. Petronelle was sitting in her usual armchair. The chair beside him was empty.

"Where am I?" he asked aloud.

Petronelle rose without haste, put her sewing aside, and came over to the bed.

"Why, you're in New Nerra, Keelin," she said, laying the back of her hand on his forehead, then pressing her fingers to his wrist to check his pulse. "In the best guest bedroom of the chieftain's lodge."

He stared at her, bewildered. "New Nerra" struck

some sort of chord in his mind, though very faintly. "Keelin" meant something to him, too, of course. He had heard Petronelle say the name many times. It was *his* name, it seemed. But . . .

"Keelin," he murmured, testing the sound on his tongue.

His nurse shrugged, looking embarrassed. "Oh, I know that's not your real name," she said. "But I had to call you something, didn't I? I've been boxed up in here with you for five whole days."

"Five . . ." He felt a stab of pure panic.

Time is short. . . .

He should not be lying here. There was something he had to do. Something vitally important.

"Now, don't you fret," Petronelle scolded as he started up on his pillows. "You'll make yourself ill again and undo all my good work! So what *is* your name? Can you tell me?" She tilted her head to one side, and waited.

He thought. Nothing came to him.

"No," he said bleakly. "I cannot remember it. I cannot remember anything! Only running to Zak and the beast . . ."

A shadow flickered in the old woman's strange, odd-colored eyes, but her smile remained in place. "Never mind," she said comfortably. "It'll all come back to you soon enough, and in the meantime, you can be Keelin. It means 'young dragon,' so it suits you. Brave as a dragon, you were at Fell End, and that's the truth."

She pulled the covers back in a bustling way that stopped him saying any more. "Now, let's get you out of bed for a while. That'll do you good. And I'll wager you're hungry as a dragon, too!"

In a few minutes "Keelin" was sitting by an empty fireplace, next to the window he had watched from his bed for so long. The sea breeze was cool on his flushed face, but he was warm in a striped cotton dressing gown, with a light blanket over his knees.

A fragrant smell rose from the corner of the room where Petronelle was clattering dishes. In the darkness of the fireplace, something chattered and squeaked. Keelin caught a glimpse of a twitching pink nose.

Clink, he thought, and was absurdly pleased to have remembered the word.

As he leaned forward in his chair to see the little creature more clearly, something crackled in the pocket of the striped gown.

Curiously he pushed his hand into the pocket and drew out a scrap of paper. It seemed to be a message of some kind. He blinked at it, the angrily scrawled words blurring before his eyes.

THEY CALL YOU A HERO, KEELIN, BUT I KNOW WHO AND WHAT YOU REALLY ARE. LEAVE HERE NOW, YOU FILTHY TRAITOR, OR I SWEAR ON MY SOUL YOU WILL REGRET IT.

KEELIN

Fighting down a wave of sickness, the boy whose name for now was Keelin crumpled the threatening note in his fist. *Who am I?* he thought frantically. *What have I done to make someone hate me so much?* His head began to swim. He shut his eyes, ordering himself to relax.

And as his mind steadied, he realized with grim amusement that he had learned something new about himself, at least.

He was not used to being hated. Not like this. Not so personally. Otherwise, the loathing in the message would not have shocked him so badly. Whoever he was, he had been used to being liked — even loved.

So he did not need to fear. Deliberately he opened his eyes, smoothed out the paper, and read the words again. This time, he took in the points that should have struck him from the beginning.

The writer of the message thought he was only pretending to have lost his memory. The writer knew him. And the writer had been in this room, for how else could the message have been placed in the pocket of the gown?

Keelin's thoughts ran on, suddenly clear as a bubbling stream.

He had a secret enemy. If he could unmask that enemy, he would get what he most wanted — knowledge of who he was, and, with luck, what he should be doing.

Petronelle turned and began stumping toward him, carrying a steaming bowl. Hastily, Keelin stuffed the note back into his gown pocket. He did not want her to see it, to exclaim, to make a fuss. He wanted to think about the problem in peace, at least for now.

Murmuring his thanks, he took the bowl of rice porridge sprinkled with dried berries and drizzled with honey.

Petronelle peered at him. "You're looking a bit feverish," she said, frowning.

"I am well," he assured her, and took a spoonful of the sweet, gluey porridge to prove it.

Petronelle waited till he had taken another spoonful, then whisked away to pull open the door of the apartment.

Watching from his chair, Keelin was surprised to see that a strapping young man with a scarred face was standing on guard outside the door.

"Jett, please tell Chieftain Farr that the patient is awake," Petronelle said crisply.

The man nodded sullenly and marched away.

Petronelle closed the door again with a slight flounce. She looked around and saw her patient staring, the spoon halfway to his lips.

"I had to tell, Keelin," she said. "I swore to Farr that I would."

"I did not know this room was guarded," said Keelin. "Is that to keep me in, or to keep others out?"

The old woman shrugged. "A bit of both, I daresay. Eat up!" She went to his bed and began straightening the covers with sharp, cross little tugs.

Keelin ate a little more porridge. It was very good. The clink in the fireplace chattered, and he threw it a scrap of dried fruit.

"That guard — Jett — did not seem friendly," he ventured.

"He's not," snapped Petronelle. "Not to me, in any case. It's my eyes."

She turned away from the bed. In the light streaming from the window, the difference between her two eyes, one green, one brown, was very noticeable.

"The mismatch happens in my family from time to time," she said. "Some say it's a curse because of a wrongdoing long ago, but I don't know about that. Maybe it's always been."

"I think it is interesting," Keelin said loyally,

tossing another scrap to the clink. "Jett is a fool to dislike you because of the color of your eyes!"

The woman smiled without humor. "He's not the only one. Finish your breakfast, Keelin. Farr will be here soon. And stop feeding that clink!"

She turned back to the bed. Keelin ate the last of his porridge and put the empty bowl on the floor. He felt restless and uneasy. Suddenly the familiar room seemed more like a prison than a refuge.

On impulse, he pushed the blanket aside and stood up, holding on to the arm of the chair for support. His bare feet felt tender on the wooden floor. His legs were wobbly. He glanced guiltily at Petronelle, but she still had her back turned. He edged to the window, leaned on the deep sill, and looked down.

He was high above the ground. The street below was broad and busy. Horse-drawn carts clattered to and fro in the center. People strolled by on either side, stopping now and then to look in the windows of the shops that lined the road. Wooden barrels planted with flowers stood by many of the shop doors. Everything looked very clean, very bright, and totally unfamiliar.

Voices whispered in Keelin's mind. His eyes watered in the sunlight. As he straightened, he caught sight of his own reflection in the window glass — a ghostly face framed with a broad strip of white bandage. He turned away from it, reaching blindly for his chair, and winced as he trod on something small and hard.

He looked down to see what had hurt him. It looked like a bead — part of an earring, perhaps. Taking care not to lose his balance, he bent and picked it up.

It was a pebble — a bright blue pebble. He looked down at it, cupped in his palm. It stirred something in him — something deep and very powerful.

He felt a thrill of excitement. The pebble meant something. For some reason, it made him feel strong, warm, and safe. But how had it come here? And when? Every evening, just before settling him for the night, Petronelle swept the floor. She did it thoroughly, chasing down every crumb, thread, and speck of dust. She would not have missed a pebble.

So the pebble had come in the night. Either someone had come into the room while he and Petronelle were sleeping, or . . .

Keelin looked back at the window — the window that was always left open at night. He imagined the pebble sailing into the room, thrown by someone standing in the street below.

There was a knock on the door, which at once snapped open. Startled, Keelin lurched back into his chair, stuffing the pebble deep into the pocket of his gown with the threatening note.

Chieftain Farr and the lady Janna entered the room. Zak was with them, tiptoeing cautiously as if he had been warned to be very quiet. Petronelle swung around from the bed, and by the time the door had shut, she was hovering protectively by Keelin's side.

"Never fear, Petronelle," Farr said with a tired smile. "We were at breakfast, so came along together, but we will not trouble your patient too long. I merely wish to know —"

"He still remembers nothing," the old woman said bluntly. "Not so much as his own name, let alone anything else. But it will come." She glanced at Keelin, and he nodded, his heart sinking as he saw the disappointment in Farr's eyes.

"I am sorry," he said. "I have tried, but . . ."

"Do not apologize!" Farr said, moving forward and stretching out his hand. "It is we who should apologize to you! You were hurt saving our son! And for that I can only thank you, from the bottom of my heart."

Keelin took the offered hand. "I am sure you would do the same for me," he murmured, then felt awkward as he saw Farr and Janna exchange puzzled glances as if his reply seemed a little strange to them.

They do not say that here, he thought suddenly. *They reply to thanks in a different way.* And silently he added another fact to his small store. He was a stranger in this place. A foreigner.

Yet he did not feel like a foreigner. Until this moment, he had thought he was one with these people. A lost one, certainly, but not a stranger.

Zak was whispering to his mother. At her nod, he moved forward and gravely presented Keelin with something wrapped in a white napkin. The gift proved to be a small brown cake that smelled of spices.

"Thank you, Zak," Keelin said. "I will enjoy that later."

"You're welcome," the child said, then added, with a sly grin, "I mean . . . I'm sure you'd do the same for me."

Janna smiled. Keelin's heart warmed.

"Was there nothing in his possessions that might identify him?" Farr asked Petronelle as she carried away the spice cake and put it on the shelf where she kept her supply of food.

Keelin saw the old woman's eyes slide quickly to the chest in the corner of the room and just as quickly slide away again as she shook her head.

"At last your memory will return, Keelin, I am sure of it," Janna said gently. "It is best you do not strain yourself to remember."

"Sometimes another shock or blow will do it," said Petronelle, returning to Keelin's side. She frowned at Zak, who had leaned forward with interest. "Not," she added forcefully, "that this should be tried. It may do more harm than good."

There was another knock on the door. The door opened a little, and Jett's face appeared in the gap.

"Councilors Manx, Sigrid, and Barron are here, Chieftain Farr," Jett said, his scarred face expressionless. "They say the matter is urgent."

Farr nodded shortly. Petronelle began to protest, but he quelled her with a glance.

"Farr —" Janna murmured.

Farr shook his head. "I must hear what they have to say, Janna, and I can't do it in the hallway. Besides, they will know by now that Keelin is awake. They will have asked Jett, and he would see no reason to lie."

Keelin watched alertly as three people came through the door — a thin, black-robed man; a stout, red-faced man; and a very upright woman with a gray braid wound around her head. As Farr introduced them to him, Keelin could feel their suspicion and dislike. Or perhaps the dislike flowed from only one of them. He could not tell.

"Has the boy's memory returned?" asked the stout man Farr had called Barron.

As Farr shook his head, the other man, Manx, frowned. "We have news from the inland," he said. He glanced at Petronelle, Zak, and Janna, clearly unwilling to talk in front of them.

"Petronelle, would you please take Zak back to our rooms and see that he finishes his breakfast?" Farr asked easily.

Shooting Manx a scathing look, Petronelle took Zak by the hand and left the room, squeezing past Jett, who was still hovering in the open doorway. Janna stood her ground, smiling pleasantly as if she was entirely unaware that Manx wanted her gone.

"Yes, Jett?" Farr asked as the guard made no move to shut the door.

Jett held out an envelope. "This came for you a few minutes ago, sir," he said, moving into the room. "I did not want to disturb you, but you may wish to take it now."

Farr took the envelope, glanced at it, and suppressed a sigh.

"A message from Carryl," he said to his wife as Jett retreated, closing the door behind him.

Manx looked sour. Sigrid sighed. Barron turned down the corners of his mouth in comical dismay. "Open it, Farr!" he groaned. "Let's see what the old girl has to say this time."

With obvious reluctance, Farr pulled a note from the envelope. The writing was large and spiky. Keelin could easily read it from where he sat.

My dear Farr,
I write in haste. Rumor has it that you may give the order to attack at any moment. You know my feelings, so I will not repeat them here. I only beg that you will stay your hand at least until you have spoken to me once more.
Last night, I made an important discovery. It is vital you see it before taking a step that may be disastrous for us all. Please come to the museum as soon as you are able.
In faith, Carryl

THE CHEST

With a rueful glance at his wife, Farr refolded the note and put it back into its envelope. Then he pushed the envelope deep into his jacket pocket. If he had hoped that by removing it from his councilors' sight he would discourage them from remarking on it, he was disappointed.

"The same old story," sneered Manx. "By the stars, the woman never gives up!"

"Carryl deserves our respect," Sigrid said stiffly. "She was a great chieftain in her day."

"Indeed she was," Barron agreed. "But she's . . . well, she's very old now, Sigrid, and her mind's not as clear as it once was. Her obsession with that shambles she calls a museum and what might lie beneath it —"

"There is nothing wrong with Carryl's mind!" Janna broke in. "She just sees things differently from other people."

"Yes." Manx smiled thinly. "And that is because she buries her head in the sand in more ways than one. Carryl has never seen a slay. She has never heard the screams of beasts caught outside shelter. She has never seen words of terror scarred in a field, the crop withered as if by a freezing hand."

"And she still refuses to believe the stories of beings that prowl at night, setting fires and attacking innocents," Barron added, his jowls trembling with earnestness. "She calls them rumors and fishermen's tales, when we all know they're true."

Farr glanced at Keelin and frowned. "This isn't the time or place to be discussing Carryl," he said. "What news do you have for me?"

"There were hundreds of slays over Fell End and the surrounding farms last night," Sigrid said in a low voice. "Five Riverside people were found this morning dead in their beds for no apparent reason. And there was another message burned into a tarny field halfway to New Nerra."

"And it said?" Farr demanded.

Barron shrugged, fiddling with the gold earring in his left ear. "Oh, the usual," he muttered. " 'Prepare to Die!' Our enemy has no imagination."

"This is no joking matter!" snapped Manx. "Farr — the pipeline will be completed tomorrow and the people want you to act! They cannot understand your dithering! They have all heard of the attack on your son. They cannot understand why even that was not enough to move you. They see it as weakness!"

"That can't be helped!" Farr snapped. "I can't act blindly! I have to find out more before taking a step that can't be reversed!"

"It's a big decision," agreed Barron. "And it'll be a brave man who makes it. I'm glad it's not up to me."

Sigrid curled her lip. "I daresay you are. Especially since delay suits you, Trader Barron. After all, you are very fond of money, and the longer the slay attacks go on, the more slay shields you sell."

"Sigrid, that was unforgiveable!" Farr barked as the red in Barron's cheeks darkened to purple.

Barron raised his chin. "You wrong me, Sigrid of Gold Marsh," he said with surprising dignity. "I sell slay shields, certainly, but nothing would please me more than to be able to throw all my remaining stock into the sea!"

"I apologize," the woman said stiffly. "I spoke hastily. This morning's news upset me and I — am not myself. But I cannot see the sense in waiting once we are ready to strike. The Enemy has ignored our appeals, our demands, and our threats. Not one of our messengers has returned to us. All are dead, I fear."

"Indeed. Six brave hearts sacrificed for nothing," Barron mumbled. Suddenly he looked much older.

Farr took a deep breath. "We're all under great strain, friends, but I beg you to be patient. Petronelle is sure Keelin's memory will return, given time. And she's sure he knows something important."

"You put too much faith in Petronelle," Manx said, scowling. "She may be your wife's old nurse, and the nurse of your son, but this does not mean she can be trusted in all things. Any fool can see she has Fellan blood! Those eyes —"

"Many of Dorne's old families have a trace of Fellan blood," Janna retorted hotly. "It may run in your own veins, Trader Manx, for all you know!"

Manx's thin face darkened in anger.

"Petronelle's loyalty is beyond question!" Janna rushed on. "I bless the day my parents chose her to be my nurse. They, at least, had no foolish fears of Fellan blood!"

"Your mother and father were not born here, Lady Janna," Sigrid remarked, inspecting the rings on her fingers. "They could not be expected to understand our history."

Janna looked at her with dislike. "My parents may have been born across the sea, Councilor Sigrid, but Dorne was the home of my ancestors. Despite what you tried to claim when you were standing against Farr for election as chieftain, my family's links with this island are as ancient as his or yours — more ancient, perhaps! Not that it should matter to anyone with sense!"

"Oh, very true!" Barron chattered anxiously. "I'm sure it doesn't matter a jot to most people that your parents were foreigners, Lady. I deal with foreigners every day in the way of business, and some are very fine fellows!"

Seeing that Janna did not look in the least soothed, he blundered on. "And as for part-Fellan — well, I don't suppose there's much harm in most of them. As long as they're watched, you know."

"You should ask yourself some hard questions, Farr!" Manx hissed, ignoring Janna and Barron and glancing coldly at Keelin. "What better way for a spy to worm his way into a chieftain's confidence than to stage a rescue of that chieftain's only child? How do you know this boy has lost his memory at all? How do you know that this whole affair is not an enemy plot to keep you dangling and hesitating, waiting for information that will never come?"

"Steady on, old fellow," Barron protested.

Manx shot him a disgusted look.

"I am not a spy!" Keelin cried, unable to keep silent any longer. "I have truly lost my memory — lost myself! My mind is a mass of shadows. I hate it! I swear to you, if I could remember, I would!"

"So you say," Manx sneered, turning away. "And while you wander in the shadows, it seems, the whole of Dorne must wait."

By the time his visitors left, Keelin was gray with exhaustion. He dozed in his chair for the rest of the day, his nurse frowning over her sewing by the window.

Only as evening fell did he rouse himself and begin thinking of all that had passed that morning.

"Did Manx, Sigrid, or Barron visit me while I was ill?" he asked Petronelle, trying to sound merely curious.

The old woman snorted. "All of them came at one time or another," she said, carrying a bowl of noodles and vegetables to his chair and handing him a spoon. "None of them believed you were as badly injured as you were, I could see that. I daresay they all think you and I have hatched a plot between us, and that you are an enemy spy."

Keelin did not tell her that Manx, at least, certainly held that view. He merely nodded and went on thinking as he picked at his food, throwing scraps to the clink whenever Petronelle turned her back. So, any one of the three councilors could have put the hateful message in his dressing-gown pocket.

Despite his lazy day, he fell asleep easily when it was time. But in the middle of the night, he woke, as suddenly as if someone had whispered in his ear. Moonlight was filtering through the thin curtain that covered the window. Faint snores were rising from Petronelle's narrow cot.

Keelin slid out of bed. The clink in the fireplace chattered, and he glanced quickly at Petronelle, afraid the sound would wake her.

He still had not eaten the cake Zak had given him. Petronelle had left it on the table beside the bed in case he felt hungry in the night. With a mental apology to Zak, Keelin snatched up the cake and padded over to the fireplace.

"Here," he whispered, putting the cake down on the hearth. "Now be quiet!"

The clink, a pale glimmer in the gloom, gave one excited squeak as if it could not believe its luck. Then tiny claws grasped the treat and dragged it back into the shadows.

Wasting no time, Keelin crept to the chest in the corner and cautiously raised the lid. Inside were some neatly folded clothes, a cracked belt, and a battered pair of boots. He knelt by the chest and took out the garments one by one.

They were all very worn, but they had been washed, dried, and pressed so they smelled faintly of soap and sunshine. There was nothing in any of the pockets. The clothes told him nothing. He might never have seen them in his life before.

Fighting bitter disappointment, he lifted out the boots. As he did, something that had been jammed between them and the side of the chest rolled clear.

It was a stick — just an ordinary, smooth stick. Dimly he recalled Zak pressing a stick into his hands during the night on the barge. And had Petronelle not told him that he had run to save the boy with only a stick for a weapon? This must be the very stick! Petronelle had taken it from him at some point and put it away with everything else.

Curiously, Keelin reached for it. And the moment his fingers closed around it, a memory surged into his mind so violently that he almost cried out.

Crashing waves. The sun burning like fire as it melted into the horizon. Glittering beasts — sea serpents — their terrible, dripping heads and long, spiked necks swaying above the heaving sea . . .

Keelin leaned, panting against the open chest, his head whirling. What did this mean? Where had this memory come from?

But he knew. He knew by the familiar way the stick fitted his hand that he had held it many times before. It was not a makeshift weapon he had snatched up at Fell End, but part of his lost past.

Vainly he struggled to recall more. Dull pain thudded behind his eyes. He shut it out and thought of the beast at Fell End, concentrating on the stick, on the smoothness of the stick. What had happened in the moments before he ran to Zak? What had he seen?

Remember! he urged himself. *Prove to Manx and the others that you are no traitor!*

Shapes moved sluggishly in the dimness of his mind. None would move into the light.

Hot tears of frustration burned in his eyes. He thrust the stick back into the chest, and was doing the same with the boots when he jumped. His rough handling had dislodged something that had been stuffed into the toe of the left boot. Slowly he pulled it out.

It was a strangely shaped piece of gray fabric,

very light and fine. He knew at once what it was. It was a hood — and it belonged to him, he was sure of it. But why had it been jammed into the toe of the boot?

An answer came to him, and his heart gave a great thud. Cautiously he tipped the boot and gave it a little shake. With a soft, sliding sound, a small drawstring bag with a long braided cord fell into his hand.

Keelin's palm tingled. His skin prickled. Warmth spread through him like flame. The bag was his, just as the hood was his, and the stick. They were more his than the clean, shabby clothes folded in the chest. He did not know why, but he knew it was so.

He opened the bag but could see little of the contents. He felt around with a trembling finger. There was a feather, he thought, and something hard and knobbly —

He fell back with a gasp, snatching his finger away as the bag lit up like a tiny lantern. In the fireplace, the clink chittered in fright, and across the room, Petronelle mumbled and half woke.

Keelin sat shaking and blinking, his eyes still dazzled by the flash of light. His head pounded ominously. He knew he had to get back to bed. It would not do for Petronelle to find him here.

For who else but Petronelle could have hidden the little bag in the toe of the boot, and used the silken hood as a plug to hold it in place? Why had she done it? And why had she not breathed a word about the bag to him or anyone else?

Quickly he pulled the drawstring tight once more and, without thinking very much about what he was doing, looped the cord around his neck, tucking the bag under his nightshirt.

Silently he closed the chest and tiptoed back to bed, the silken hood crushed in his hand. To his relief, the clink had stopped chattering and gone back to its meal. But just as he slid between the covers, he heard Petronelle yawning, then the springs of her cot squeaking as she sat up.

He lay very still, his heart pounding, as the old woman got up, poured herself a drink of water, and returned to bed. Slowly the pain in his head eased. With the hand that held the hood, he pressed the little bag to his chest. It was strangely comforting. He could just hear the small sounds of the clink scrabbling after the last of the cake crumbs in the fireplace.

He had not thought he would sleep — had not imagined sleep would be possible — but the next thing he knew, it was morning.

His head felt clear. Petronelle was still snoring gently in her corner. The drawstring bag was warm against his chest. Now was the time to examine its contents.

He slid out of bed, put on the striped dressing gown, and padded across the room. Dawn light was seeping through the curtain. There was another blue pebble on the floor beneath the window. And the clink in the fireplace was dead.

CARRYL

Petronelle started up when Keelin cried out. She jumped out of bed and hurried over to him, plump in her pink, frilled nightgown, her fluffy hair standing up at odd angles all over her head. She clicked her tongue when she saw the small, cold body on the hearth. The clink had clearly been lying there for hours. Its tiny claws were spread wide, its mouth was gaping, the sooty flaps of skin that Keelin recognized with surprise and pity as sad little wings had stiffened in death.

"Ah, never mind, Keelin," Petronelle soothed. "Poor creature. Its time had come, that's all."

She went to the door, looked out, and murmured something. Instantly Jett was in the room. He strode to the fireplace and removed the dead clink, wrapping it first in a piece of rag the old woman thrust at him.

"I gave it the spice cake last night," Keelin said,

the moment the door had closed again. "The spice cake that was meant for me."

Petronelle stared at him. Suddenly her face was watchful.

"You think it was poisoned," she said slowly. "But Zak gave it to you. Surely you do not think he or Farr —?"

Keelin shook his head. On impulse, he took the threatening message from his pocket and handed it to her. She read it in silence, rubbing her mouth with the back of her hand.

The drawstring bag seemed to throb against Keelin's skin. The silken hood and the two blue pebbles burned in the pocket of his gown. He opened his mouth to speak — to ask about the hiding of the bag, the hood. . . .

"Listen to me, Keelin," Petronelle whispered, leaning toward him. "This is very important." She swallowed. "I've tried to protect you, but now that it's known you're awake and gaining strength, I'll have less and less power over what happens to you. You're going to have to find your own way, and if you can't remember what that way is, you're just going to have to trust your instincts to lead you right."

Keelin gaped at her in confusion.

"I know you're good," she went on, in the same low whisper. "You can't nurse someone for as long as I've nursed you and not know his heart. You're kind, Keelin. You're brave. You're loving. You think things through. You try to do what's right. You wouldn't willingly harm any living creature."

She was very sincere, Keelin could feel it. But her words of praise, which should have warmed him, made him uneasy. For why had she said them at all?

"I feel it was meant that we should meet," the harsh old voice whispered on. "I think perhaps it's why I was born. I've betrayed Farr and Janna for you, Keelin. I haven't told them all I know. I've kept some things secret, till your memory came back and you could speak for yourself."

"Petronelle —" Keelin began, but she shook her head and put her fingers to his lips.

"No, there's more," she hissed. "We haven't much time — I feel it! It's been hard for me, very hard, to make myself deceive Farr and Janna. Farr's a fine man, and Janna's like my own child. I pray I've done right. Swear to me that whatever the future holds you'll do nothing to harm them, Keelin! Swear to help Farr in his struggle. Swear to be loyal to him, to the death!"

She took her fingers away. Her strange eyes searched Keelin's, filled with agonized appeal.

"I swear it with all my heart," Keelin said without hesitation, and watched with wondering pity as the old woman's face became slack with relief. She had asked so little of him. How could he ever regret such an oath? He had nothing but respect for Chieftain Farr, wanted nothing more than to help him.

Petronelle turned away and hurried to her cot. She threw a red dressing gown over her nightdress, smoothed her hair, and thrust her feet into worn slippers.

"I'm going to Farr and Janna, to tell them about the clink," she whispered, going to the door. "There's no time to lose if I'm to catch them alone. Lock the door after me, Keelin. Open to no one but Janna, Farr, or me. And, Keelin — keep your bandage on! Whatever you may think, you need it!"

And with that, she was gone.

Keelin locked the door after her, feeling more confused and helpless than ever. He looked over his shoulder at his rumpled bed, suddenly yearning to lie down, draw the covers up to his chin, and sleep.

But another part of his mind was resisting — the part that was tired of confusion and helplessness, the part that was telling him it was time to be himself again, with memory or without it.

He walked to the window and drew back the curtain. The sky was clear, pale blue. He stood for a moment, taking great gulps of air that smelled of the sea. Then he left the window and moved past the silent fireplace to the chest in the corner.

He opened the chest and slowly dressed himself, pulling garments out one at a time. At last, only the stick remained. He picked it up cautiously, but this time there was no disturbing flash of memory, only a feeling of rightness. He pushed it into his belt, and at once knew that was where it belonged.

Fully clothed for the first time in days, his feet unnaturally heavy in boots, he went to his chair and sat down. He was tired, but as he had hoped, dressing had made him feel less like an invalid and more like a person who could control his own destiny.

He put his hand over the little bag that hung around his neck. *Now,* he thought, *I am ready to think about you.* But before he could open the drawstring, there was a violent hammering on the door.

"Open, Keelin!" Farr shouted, his voice harsh with fear. "For pity's sake, make haste! I need you!"

❋

Ten minutes later, Keelin was rattling through the city in a carriage with Zak by his side. Jett was in front, driving the horses, but otherwise they were alone. It was so early that few people were on the streets, and they sped along at a good pace.

"The museum's good to visit," Zak told his companion happily. "It's very old. People always want to pull it down but Carryl won't let them."

Keelin smiled and nodded, though he had barely heard what the child had said. His mind was back at the chieftain's lodge where Petronelle, grim-faced, was laboring to save the lady Janna, who was lying still and pale like one dead.

"If Petronelle hadn't knocked on our door and roused me when she did, it would have been too late!" Farr had said through chattering teeth. "I woke to find Janna barely breathing. Poisoned, Keelin, like the clink in your room! As it is, there's a chance. If anyone can save her, it's Petronelle."

Zak did not know his mother's danger. Zak thought only that he was being given a great treat — an unexpected visit to the museum with Keelin.

"I must get the boy away," Farr had muttered rapidly. "He mustn't know what's happened — not yet. He'll suffer enough later if — if things don't go well."

He had swallowed and quickly turned his head away, and suddenly, Keelin had been gripped by a vivid memory of someone else — someone he saw in his mind only as a quick flash. Someone tall and strong, with a great heart and powerful emotions he tried not to show. Frantically, Keelin had groped after the image, trying to call it back, but it had gone.

"Till I get to the bottom of this horror you're the only one I can trust to go with Zak, Keelin, for you were almost a victim of the poisoner yourself," Farr had gone on after a moment. "If I send him alone with Jett, he'll know there's something wrong. But if I tell him *you* want to see the museum . . ."

The carriage was slowing. And there before them was a deep, sparkling bay, edged by a low stone wall.

His interest roused in spite of his fears, Keelin drank in the sight. The bay was crowded with ships and surrounded by docks and warehouses. Even at this early hour, the decks of the ships were alive with movement. On the shore, pie sellers and vendors of sweet buns, soup, coffee, and tea were already at work, serving the gaudily clad customers clustering around their stalls.

Standing at the top of a small rise straight ahead, commanding a magnificent view of the bay, was a low ramshackle building.

"We're here!" cried Zak as the carriage came to a stop. "Come on, Keelin! Carryl will be so glad to see us! She says more people should come to the museum. She says people don't realize how important it is, and that's why the council won't vote for money to mend it. But Father and Mother understand. They say the museum should stay here, whatever Trader Manx and Trader Barron think."

He glanced at Keelin anxiously, perhaps suddenly realizing how shabby the museum was and fearing that the visitor might be disappointed.

"I am looking forward to seeing inside," Keelin said heartily, though in truth the old building looked like a wreck to him. He could well understand why the traders whose warehouses stood around the bay might envy its prime position and see it as a blot on the landscape. It was hard to imagine that there would be anything much to see in such a place.

But it would be interesting to meet Carryl, beloved chieftain-turned-museum-keeper. Interesting, too, to hear about the "important discovery" Carryl had mentioned in her message to Farr. Wishing his legs were not quite so wobbly, Keelin followed Zak up the little hill, leaving Jett staring broodingly out to sea.

Wearing filthy overalls, heavy gloves, and work boots, Carryl greeted her visitors in a small, dusty lobby that smelled vaguely of cooked vegetables. She was extremely tall and thin, with a beaky nose; a wide, humorous mouth; piercing blue eyes; and white hair screwed into a tiny knot on the top of her head. Old as she was, her every movement seemed charged with energy. Beside her was a puny boy, a few years younger than Zak, whose features were miniature versions of hers, giving his small face a clownish look.

"Pieter, take Zak into the workroom and find that tin of sweet cakes your mother sent," Carryl said as the two boys eyed each other without speaking. "You can have one each. Go along!"

His shyness forgotten, Pieter dashed to the back of the lobby, threw open a door marked "No Entry," and beckoned wildly to Zak. "Cakes!" he yelled. "Come see! An' then I'll show you the giant's head cutter Carryl found, from the olden days!"

Zak followed slowly, making it clear that he was the older of the two, and that neither sweet cakes nor head cutters were of particular interest to him.

"Pieter's my youngest grandson," Carryl said, stripping off her gloves and ushering Keelin into a large, echoing room where cracked bowls, broken daggers, and other sad objects were ranged on sagging shelves. "He spends a lot of time here with me — he likes old things and old tales. The others tease him because he's small for his age, but I tell him he'll likely shoot up in time like I did and be bigger than any of them one day. Now . . ."

She closed the door and turned her sharp blue gaze on her companion.

"So you're the one who saved Zak — the one who's lost his memory. You look as if you should still be in bed! Why did Farr send you instead of coming himself? What's happened?"

Keelin told her. The corners of her mouth tightened.

"First Zak, now Janna," she muttered. "By the stars, how much more can Farr take before he cracks and lets the council have its way? I've got to work faster. But how can I? I'm here twenty-four hours a day as it is! If only I could get more help!"

She grimaced at Keelin's expression.

"Don't think I don't care about Janna. I care, all right. But I've lived a long time and I've learned to put feelings aside when I have to. And for now there's nothing more important than stopping Farr launching his attack when there's another way."

"Another . . . ?"

"Another way, yes! I feel it! I *know* it! Here!"

She grabbed Keelin's arm and dragged him back into the lobby and through the door marked "No Entry." The two boys were standing at the far end of the cluttered workroom beyond, eating cake and arguing loudly.

"It's not a head cutter!" Zak was saying scornfully. "It's just a rusty old tool like farmers use for cutting stalks to feed the hogs."

"A head cutter!" Pieter insisted.

"Whatever it is, don't touch it!" Keelin shouted. He had no time to say more. The next moment Carryl had thrown back a curtain and hauled him through another doorway, into a room without windows.

Here all the central floorboards had been pried away, and a great black hole yawned, exuding the smell of ancient rock and sour, damp earth. Keelin felt a stab of panic.

"Down there," the old woman cried, pointing into the stinking darkness. "That's where the answer lies — the proof I need to convince Farr, to convince them all! The spirits tell me so!"

And at that moment, in terror, Keelin heard someone shouting in his mind — shouting the same words, over and over again.

Get out! Get out! Get out!

Then there was an explosion as loud as a hundred thunderclaps. For one wild moment, Keelin thought the building had been struck by lightning, then he remembered that the sky had been clear. The ceiling above him fell. He dropped to his knees, covering his head. Shattered plaster rained down on him, great beams crashed around him. He heard Carryl scream, and his blood ran cold.

The deafening roar faded away, but the old building was creaking and groaning ominously. The walls were shaking. Terrified wails were coming from the workroom.

"Pieter," Carryl called feebly. "Zak . . ."

Keelin staggered to his feet and in a blink had reached the workroom.

The two boys were crouched together halfway to the door, plaster swirling like fine rain around them. Pieter had fallen. Zak was struggling to pull him up. Keelin seized them both, one in each arm, and sped them out of the workroom, through the lobby, and out into the air. How he moved with such speed he had no idea. He never gave the ring on his finger a single thought.

"Zak, get Pieter away!" he ordered, and plunged back for Carryl.

She was lying where he had left her, a vast beam across her chest, pinning her down.

"Pieter . . ." she murmured as Keelin struggled to free her.

"Outside. Safe. With Zak."

Her eyes closed in relief. "Pocket," she croaked. "Book. For Farr. Then go. Go!"

There was a low rumbling sound. Straining timbers squeaked and cracked.

Get out! Get out! Get out!

"I cannot — leave — you," Keelin gasped, struggling with the beam, refusing to listen to the voice screaming in his mind, though his head felt as if it was bursting.

Carryl's eyes fluttered open. They fixed him with a stern gaze. It seemed to him that the blue was already fading.

Sweat broke out on her forehead as, with her one free hand, she fumbled in the pocket of her overalls and pulled out a small book with a faded leather cover. Her cracked lips opened. The voice came, harsh with pain but full of authority.

"I am finished. Save the book! Get it to Farr! Tell him to . . ."

And that was all. The words died on her lips as her brave heart gave up its struggle and her pain ended.

Shaking, Keelin pulled the book from the dead fingers. Turning to run, he looked down at the title, printed in gold on the front.

The Three Brothers

He stared at the title, transfixed.
It is going! GET OUT!

There was a groaning crash. The rumbling mounted to a roar. Clutching the book, Keelin took a single step toward the doorway. And then the floor gave way beneath his feet, and the world collapsed in on him.

THE PIT

He woke in the dark. He woke to raging thirst, to the smell of dust and decay, to a sense of ancient evil so strong that for a time he could only lie shivering without thought, listening to the sound of his own ragged breaths. Then slowly, slowly, his mind began to work. Little by little he remembered what had happened to him, where he was . . .

And who he was.

"Rye," he whispered aloud. Suddenly his time as Keelin, the stranger, seemed like a dream. The shadows that had darkened his memory were still there, but they were clearing in patches that broadened every moment.

Sonia, Rye thought. *Dirk. Sholto. Where are they? Why did they not come for me? Are they safe?* The wings of terror fluttered briefly at the edges of his mind, but he brushed them away. He could not afford weakness now. And surely he would know if Sonia, Dirk, and Sholto were in danger or dead.

Cautiously he moved one hand, then the other. He tested his feet, his legs. He sat up, wincing at the pain in his head, and the light debris that had covered him fell away in a chinking, rattling shower.

He felt for the bell tree stick. By a miracle, it was still in his belt, and unbroken. In another moment, he had found that the bag of powers, too, was safe.

The wave of warmth these discoveries gave him did not last long. Soon the evil-smelling darkness was pressing in on him again, and his skin was crawling at the thought of what might be lurking within it. He pulled the light crystal from the bag. Its brilliance was a blessing, but so dazzling that at first he had to shield his eyes. Squinting through slitted fingers, he peered around him.

He had fallen onto a heap of dust and ash thick with small, blackened twists of metal and crumbling objects that looked horribly like human bones. Grimy stone walls rose all around him. It was like being at the bottom of a huge well.

His stomach churning, he looked up and saw a jumble of wood and stone wedged into place high above his head.

Then he understood. He had fallen into a great pit in the ancient foundations of the museum — a burial pit, by the looks of things. Now that his eyes had become accustomed to the light he could see that some of the metal pieces looked like belt buckles, buttons, and a brooch that might once have fastened a cloak. Beside him was a round object that he feared was the top of a skull. Gingerly he touched it and it crumbled into dust very similar to the dust on which he sat.

Shuddering, Rye looked up again. Part of a wall had fallen over the top of the pit, sealing it and so protecting him when the rest of the building collapsed.

There were small gaps in the seal — places where wood crisscrossed, and massive stones lay at an angle. He could squeeze through one of those gaps, he was sure of it. But who knew what was above? There might be nothing but more stones, more huge beams, and no way of escape. But he had to find out, for what other hope did he have?

Rye took the feather from the bag. As he shakily crawled to his feet, something that had been lying beneath him caught his eye. It was the little book that Carryl had pulled from her pocket — the book she had begged him with her dying breath to save. He had forgotten it. But there it lay, pressed wide open, its fragile pages creased by the weight of his body.

He picked it up. An old, frayed ribbon bookmark trailed in the fold between the pages. Perhaps that was why the book had fallen open at that place. As the light of the crystal passed over it, a section seemed to leap out at him from the end of the right-hand page. Some of the words were underlined, as if Carryl had thought them particularly worthy of note.

✣   And so the great charm was forged and the chieftain, well satisfied, put it close to his heart and rode away from the forests with his bride. Once home, he ordered a gold casket to be made, and when the casket was ready, he put the charm inside it and hid it away where no enemy could find it. For all the years that followed, he guarded the secret of the hiding place jealously, telling it only to his eldest son, who was his favorite. At the end of his life, he died peacefully, believing that what he had done would keep his people safe forever. But the future was not to be as he would have wished. And so it happened that in time the secret of the hiding place was lost, and the gold casket has never been seen by human eyes from that day to this.

Rye stared, his heart beating fast. So this was what Carryl had wanted Farr to see! The tale of a lost treasure — Fellan, by the sound of it. Carryl had come to believe that the casket was hidden somewhere beneath the museum, and she had been working night and day to find it. Perhaps she hoped that Farr could use the charm inside to combat the enemy by magic, and so avoid bloodshed.

Rye could just imagine how Councilors Manx, Barron, and Sigrid would have greeted such an idea. And even Farr, fond of the old chieftain as he might have been, would surely not have been able to accept her story. Farr was a supremely practical man.

But Rye, shivering amid the bones of the long dead, haunted by the creeping sense of evil that seemed to seep from the very stones that surrounded him, knew that Carryl's claim could not be dismissed out of hand.

And he knew something else that Farr did not know. The Enemy was the Lord of Shadows.

Rye groaned aloud as all the urgency he had felt in the time before he had lost his memory came back to him in a great rush.

Why was he standing here when time was racing by — when so much time had been lost already? Farr might be even now raising his army, driven to furious action at last by the attack on the museum, Zak's narrow escape, and Carryl's death. Almost certainly, he believed that "Keelin" was dead, too.

Rye's stomach churned. He had to get to Farr — tell Farr what he knew. He had to stop the attack that could lead only to disaster.

As he snapped the book shut, the title written in gold on the front cover seemed to wink at him slyly. *The Three Brothers*. No wonder that title had stirred him when he first saw it! The coincidence still gave him a strange feeling. How could he have forgotten he was one of three?

Yet somehow he had forgotten. For the long days of his illness, he had been Keelin, alone. And strangely, despite his physical weakness and the shadows that still veiled some things in his past, he felt stronger than he had before.

He pushed the book into his pocket and held the feather high. The light of the crystal gleamed on the stone walls as he rose to the top of the pit.

He felt a slight draft on his face. It seemed to be blowing through a gap between two great blocks of stone. Cautiously, trying not to think about what would happen if the blocks shifted, he eased himself through the gap.

He found himself crouching in a small cavity in the rubble. A wedge of fallen wood and stone loomed low above his head. Every now and then, there was a slight grating sound, and dust filtered down in a tiny shower.

When Rye put the crystal gingerly to the rock above him, he could see nothing but more stone, more wood. There was no escape that way. He was buried deep. But he could still feel that tiny draft of air wafting from somewhere behind him.

Carefully he turned around. He wet his finger and felt the little breath of air cool on his skin. The draft was coming from a hole at the base of the wall of rubble, where a stone pillar had collapsed at an angle over a thick slab of rusty iron — a door that had fallen from its hinges long ago, by the look of it.

Rye lay flat, shining the crystal light through the gap. The glow was a little fainter than usual, no doubt because the iron slab weakened its magic, but the golden beam was bright enough for him to see something that made his heart leap. Beyond the gap, there was clear space and the edge of a low doorway.

He had to get through to that doorway — he had to! But the triangle framed by the pillar, some lumps of stone, and the metal door was far too small for him to squirm through.

If only I had the power to pass through solid objects, Rye thought desperately. *Or shrink at will! Or if I had the strength of a hundred men, even for a few moments, I could lift the pillar high enough to be able to slide underneath it!*

Suddenly he remembered the wrapped honey sweet — the only charm he had not yet used. Perhaps its power was strength! Bees had to be strong to work from dawn till dusk collecting pollen and carrying it back to the hive.

With rising hope, he found the sweet, unwrapped it, and slid it into his mouth. It tasted exactly like a honey sweet he might have bought any day at the Southwall market. And however hard he tried, he still could not move the pillar by so much as a hair.

At last, he gave up, wrapped the sweet again, and put it back in the bag. The sweetness of honey lingered on his tongue, but his disappointment was bitter. The air wafting through the gap beneath the pillar seemed to mock him. He turned his face away from it, fighting despair. He had no wish to die alone in this tomb, but even worse than the thought of dying were the other thoughts that were crowding into his mind.

Sonia, Dirk and Sholto, his mother, would never know what had happened to him. The quest to save Weld was lost. Farr and his people were lost. And the little bag of powers, which should have helped to save them all, was lost — buried and lost — because it had fallen into the wrong hands. His hands.

The future's in your hands . . .

Who had said that? It was Farr, talking to his workers at Fell End. Rye stirred. He looked down at his clenched fists, so grimy with dirt and ancient ash that he could hardly see the speed ring on his finger.

Magic had failed him this time. But he still had his will, and his own two hands.

Slowly, stubbornly, he began to clear away the rubble that lay between him and the gap. Of course it would be impossible to move the iron door that formed the base of the triangle, but if he could dig out some of what lay beneath the door, he might be able to press it down a little — just enough for him to squeeze between it and the pillar.

He dug. He dug till his nails were torn, his fingers were raw, and his shoulders ached with the strain of reaching forward. His mouth was as dry as sand and his eyes were stinging when at last he felt it was time to try to force the iron door down.

Without much hope, he leaned forward, placed his hands on the nearest part of the rusty surface, and pressed down with all his weight.

And the door shattered — simply shivered into dust.

For an instant, as rusty fragments showered into the hollow he had made, Rye thought the honey sweet had worked after all. Then he saw the truth. The impressive-looking door had been so eaten away by rust that it had been just a shell, held together by a miracle.

Even so, its collapse had made a difference to the fine balance of the ruins. The pillar moved, very slightly. There was an ominous rumble from above. Dust sifted down as massive blocks shifted and wood splintered beneath their weight.

Out! Get out!

Rye's heart seemed to leap into his throat. He dived into the newly enlarged gap and squirmed through it. Gasping, covered in flakes of rust, he jumped to his feet. The stone-edged doorway gaped before him, framing thick, whispering darkness.

He did not hesitate. He hurled himself into the darkness and ran. He ran, sobbing and laughing by turns, as behind him a mountain of stone caved in and again a voice, a well-remembered voice, rang in his mind, drowning all other thought.

Rye! Oh, Rye, at last! This way! This way!

THE MAZE

And so began a nightmare journey through a maze of passageways and ruined chambers echoing with moans and creeping with the sense of ancient evil. Crumbling statues shrouded in spiderweb hulked in dark alcoves in the walls. Often the way was blocked by a cave-in or a pool of black, foul-smelling water and another way would have to be found. Here and there, the dank walls were carved with the fantastic images of beasts — sea serpents, dragons, fish with wings, monsters with manes like mats of flabby seaweed. When the light of the crystal fell on them, the carvings seemed to loom from the stone, as if they were alive. And the sounds of suffering and misery, the growls of unnamed horrors, never ceased.

Do not listen to them, Rye! They are not real! They are only memories trapped in the stone. This way!

And Rye followed Sonia's voice. Clear as a crystal bell it called to him, cheering and directing him, and it never tired or wavered.

Time ceased to have any meaning. When the light of the crystal finally picked out a figure ahead, a figure emerging eerily from a patch of shadow in a wall, he thought he was dreaming.

But then the figure was running. And Sonia was there in front of him, haggard with weariness, hugging him fiercely, sobbing with joy.

There was so much to ask, so much to explain, but at first, Rye did not have the strength to speak. His throat was parched, his head was pounding, and he was trembling with weariness. He drank from Sonia's flask, then let her lead him to the dark alcove where she had waited for him. It was bare and free of spiderwebs. Rye sank gratefully into its shelter.

"I did not dare go any farther in search of you," Sonia said, sitting down beside him. "My candle had burned away, and I only had one pebble left." She opened her hand. On her palm lay a small, rounded stone, blue as the sky.

Another shadow drifted from Rye's memory. He dug into his pocket and pulled out the two pebbles he had found on the floor in the chieftain's lodge.

Sonia nodded wearily. "The rest are marking our trail out of here. Rye, why did you close your mind to me? I have not been able to sense you for days. It has been as if you were dead! Then suddenly I woke from sleep here and felt you clearly! In danger, but alive!" Her voice trembled, though clearly she was trying to seem calm.

So Rye told her, as best he could, of his memory loss, of his life as Keelin. And when he had finished, Sonia told him her side of the story.

She told of waking on the Fell End riverbank to cries of terror. She told of running, of seeing him being taken, unconscious and surrounded by guards, to Farr's barge. She told of fire, and people babbling of a beast sent by the enemy. She told of seeing Dirk and Sholto, both wounded, being carried onto the barge's deck among many others. She told of hearing that Rye was to be taken to the chieftain's lodge, and the barge chugging away, leaving her behind.

She said little of her journey to find him. But as she spoke, Rye caught glimpses of the long, dogged trek, the exhaustion, the hiding, the fear of asking for help from anyone.

In the city, she found her way to the chieftain's lodge. The gossip of passersby told her which room had been given to the stranger who had saved Zak from the beast. She called to Rye, tossed pebbles through his window two nights in a row, but still he did not respond. And then she saw him leave the lodge in a carriage driven by a scar-faced guard, and followed.

She did not see who made the blast that destroyed the museum, though she felt the danger just before it happened. In terror, she heard the explosion, saw the building's walls tilt and the roof fall. She saw the chieftain's son and another boy running from the wreckage in a cloud of dust just before the final collapse. She saw them picked up and driven away by the scar-faced guard. Later, she saw the body of an old woman carried out.

"But there was no sign of you," she said. "People were digging in the ruins — so many people that I could not get near. It seemed to me that some in the crowd were starting to look at me curiously — I look very ragged and wild by now, no doubt. But I could not bear to leave the place. I had to know. . . ."

Her voice trailed off. She bit her lip.

And the rest of her story Rye saw in pictures that flashed from her mind into his. He saw Sonia slipping away from the crowd. He saw her climbing farther up the hill to hide behind the shattered building. He saw her discovering what seemed to be the abandoned burrow of some animal.

He saw her crawling into the darkness, at first thinking only of shelter, then stumbling upon a maze of stone passages. He saw her moving on through whispering blackness, her candle flickering, blue pebbles falling from her fingers one by one.

And he saw her reaching the alcove and creeping into its shelter as her candle guttered and died.

"Then you went to sleep," he said, covering Sonia's hand with his. "Just before I woke in the pit knowing who I was, no doubt."

121

"No doubt." Sonia made a face. "I seem to be making a habit of sleeping through exciting events. But I was very tired. And this alcove . . . it sounds strange, Rye, but it makes me feel safe. When I first came upon it, it seemed to welcome me. And in here the voices in the stones are quiet."

Rye had not thought about it, but now that he did he realized Sonia was right. He could hardly hear the groans and whispers that had plagued him as he found his way here. Why should that be?

He flicked the crystal light around the small space and wondered why it was empty, when statues had stood in all the other alcoves he had seen. Then, as the soft beam swept over the floor, he thought he knew. The base of the alcove was covered not with dust, but with a thick layer of rust particles.

"Whatever once stood in here must have been made of metal instead of stone," he said slowly. "Over time, it has completely rusted away."

Sonia nodded without much interest. She was leaning back on the hard stones. She looked exhausted but very relaxed, as if finding Rye had for the moment driven all other cares from her mind.

Or as if there really is something about this alcove that gives her peace, Rye thought. His skin prickled.

"Sonia," he said abruptly, feeling in the bag hanging around his neck, "move out into the passage!"

The girl opened her eyes and blinked at him in surprise.

122

"Please!" Rye insisted, hardly able to contain his impatience. "There is something I want to try."

Staring, Sonia did as he asked. Rye turned in the cramped space. He pressed the key he had taken from the bag to the back wall of the alcove.

And with a grating sound, part of the wall swung open, revealing a small cavity in which stood a golden casket, glimmering in the crystal's light.

"What is it?" gasped Sonia. "How did you know it was here?"

Rye's heart was beating so fast that at first he could not answer. Reverently he lifted the casket out of its hiding place. The lid was exquisitely inlaid with blue stones. The swirling patterns seemed to move, one moment making pictures of sea serpents and fish, the next the shapes of ferns and trees. He swallowed.

"It is a legend. I read of it in an old book. It has been hidden here, underground, for a very long time. Carryl, the museum keeper, was trying to find it. . . ."

The casket was firmly sealed. He touched it with the tiny key, and its lock clicked. Gingerly he opened the lid.

Inside, resting on a cushion of threadbare velvet, was a disc as large as the palm of his hand and as thin as paper, its surface rippling green and blue like water in the light.

Rye heard Sonia catch her breath. He hesitated, then took the disc between his thumb and forefinger.

Magic thrilled through him. The little bag hanging around his neck seemed to pulse against his skin.

Carefully he lifted the disc. The velvet cushion collapsed into dust. The disc brightened, the ripples on its surface swirling and forming into words.

When I was born,
The spell was cast.
While I endure,
The Pledge will last.

"This is Fellan!" Sonia breathed. "It is like the writing we saw in the forest pool beyond the golden Door. But what does it mean?"

Rye's heart was racing, and so were his thoughts. Hastily he put the disc back into the casket. His fingers felt scorched. The light crystal, the little key, the concealing hood — all the powers he carried, the powers he had thought so wondrous — suddenly seemed no more than clever tricks. The power of the disc was something very different. It stirred him to the depths of his being.

"I think," he said in a low voice, "Sonia . . . I think it is the token of the ancient pledge by the Fellan not to interfere in the wider affairs of Dorne. The Fellan beyond the golden Door told us of that pledge — do you remember?"

Sonia nodded, staring at the disc in the casket.

In Rye's mind was the sudden memory of a conversation he had overheard in the city of Oltan. A man called Shim had been talking to Hass the fisherman. The Lord of Shadows, Shim had said, was angry because he had been defeated in a place called the Land of Dragons — repelled *by a magic more powerful than his own.*

"You are powerful magic," he murmured, his eyes on the disc. "But even more powerful are the beings who made you."

"What?" Sonia cried sharply. "Rye, what are you talking about?"

Rye turned to look at her. She was staring at him, her eyes dark with what looked like fear.

"The pledge must be what is stopping the Fellan from fighting the Lord of Shadows," Rye said. "If Farr returns this token to them — breaks it, perhaps, before their eyes — the oath will be dissolved."

"Farr will not venture into the Fell Zone," Sonia said, shaking her head. "People here hate and fear the Fellan. I have heard little on the streets, but I have gathered that much."

"You forget — I know Farr now!" Rye argued. "He trusts me. Sonia, why do you look like that? What is wrong?"

"I — I do not know," Sonia said in a small voice, quite unlike her own. "I just think it would be better to take the disc to the Fell Zone ourselves, without saying a word of it to anyone."

"No!" Rye said shortly. "Farr is the elected heir of that ancient chieftain who persuaded the Fellan to make their vow. The disc is his affair."

"It is no more his affair than it is ours!" Sonia snapped. "What is this obsession with Farr, Rye? He is nothing to you! You are a citizen of Weld!"

"You are a fine one to talk of that!" Rye muttered, backing out of the alcove with the gold casket in his hands. But as he and Sonia picked their way out of the maze of passages, following the trail of blue pebbles she had dropped during her lonely wanderings in search of him, he began to feel more and more uncomfortable.

In truth, his escape through the wooden Door, his time at Fell End, his days and nights spent as Keelin in the chieftain's lodge had changed him even more than his other two journeys beyond the Wall had. In truth, there was a part of him that no longer felt like a citizen of Weld, the home of his childhood, but like a citizen of Dorne. And in truth, Farr seemed more deserving of his loyalty than the Warden of Weld had ever been.

In silence, he and Sonia crawled from the underground into the waning light of evening. With a jolt of panic, Rye looked at the sky, then remembered there was no need to fear. The skimmers did not come to the city. They were only a problem inland.

The sea breezes tossed Sonia's hair into wild tangles. Rocks loomed around them, some solid, some hollow as chimneys and chattering with the clinks that had gnawed out their centers. Rye took a great breath of salty air and was filled with an overwhelming sense of relief.

"I would never have escaped that place without you, Sonia," he said. "Thank you."

"I am sure you would do the same for me," Sonia answered stiffly. Then she glanced at him sideways and her lips tweaked into a rueful smile. "I *know* you would do the same for me," she added. "So what choice did I have?"

She glanced at the little casket clutched in his hand and with a sigh pulled the red scarf from her neck.

"Here," she said, giving the scarf to Rye. "Use this to carry that wretched thing. It would be best to keep it hidden for now."

The scarf was a peace offering, Rye knew. He took it gratefully, knotted both the casket and the book from his pocket into it, and tied the small bundle firmly to his belt.

As they clambered down to the road below, they saw that people were still working in the ruins of the museum. Carryl's precious exhibits were being thrown onto the rubbish carts along with everything else.

"Rye, put on the hood," Sonia whispered, shrinking back. "It would be better if they did not see me."

Rye wanted to tell her that the workers would not trouble her once they knew she was a friend of his, but decided not to risk another argument over something so small. He pulled the hood of concealment over his head and took her arm.

"We should pack up for the night, Nils," he heard one worker say to another. "It's pointless going on."

"It was always pointless," his companion growled. "We were never going to find that Keelin. He's one of them, all right — set the explosion, then spirited himself away."

Rye froze where he stood.

"Zak said Keelin saved him and old Carryl's grandson," the first man muttered.

Nils made a disgusted sound. "The boy was so shocked he wouldn't know what happened. Probably mixed this up with that false rescue at Fell End."

The first man frowned. "The scar-faced guard said he saw a raggedy girl hanging around just before the blast went off. Other people saw her, too, afterward. Green eyes, they said."

The two men looked at each other meaningfully.

"They were in it together, you mark my words," Nils growled. "Filthy spies! And old Carryl dead! The end of an era! Still, one good thing's come out of it. Farr's had enough. He's given the order at last. The army's on the move. And he rode out himself this morning, they say, as soon as he knew his lady was out of danger. By now, he'll be in Riverside."

THE BARGE

Invisible beneath the hood, Rye and Sonia slipped through the darkening city. The main roads were thronged with people and crowded with heavily loaded carts. There was a hum of excitement in the air. Sellers of food and drink were doing a roaring trade, and fiddlers, pipers, and accordion players were making music on every corner.

The windows of the chieftain's lodge were dark. The building looked deserted, but hundreds of people had gathered outside it all the same, many waving small flags striped in red and yellow.

"You would think it was a festival instead of a war," Sonia whispered.

Rye nodded grimly. He was watching two daring children knocking on the door of the lodge. They had been playing this game for some time, but the door had remained firmly closed.

Plainly the scraps of gossip he had overheard were true. After the explosion at the museum, Farr was taking no risks. His lodge was an obvious target, so it had been locked and abandoned. Janna, Zak, and Petronelle had been sent to a secret place of shelter. Guards, councilors, and servants had gone with Farr or returned to their family homes.

It had been a relief to find out that Janna had recovered enough to be moved. But now she was out of Rye's reach. So were Petronelle and Zak. There was no one else he could trust to believe in him, to help him reach Farr quickly and easily.

"We will have to make our own way to Farr as best we can," he said to Sonia as they turned down a side street to avoid the crowd. "How far away is Riverside? The barge stopped there, but my memory of that time is very hazy."

Sonia stopped by a closed shop and with the tip of her finger drew in the dust filming the window.

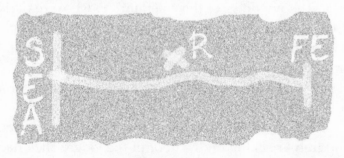

"Say this is the river," Sonia said, pointing to the wavy line she had drawn. "Here is the sea, where we are, at the beginning of the line, and here are Fell End and the Fell Zone at the end. Riverside is roughly halfway between the two — here." She pressed her finger to the spot marked *R* in her sketch.

"But why would Farr's army mass there, such a long way upriver?" Rye exclaimed.

"Why not?" Sonia shrugged. "We do not know where the Harbor is from here, Rye, and we have no idea what Farr's plan of attack is either. The famous pipeline passes Riverside — I saw it with my own eyes as I came here. It follows the river all the way to the sea like a great silver snake on stilts."

Rye frowned in puzzlement. If the pipeline was to supply drinking water for troops, why did it run to the city? It did not make sense.

He shook his head, trying to clear it. The shadows were closing in again. His memories were still very patchy. The most frustrating gap of all was the blank space just before the beast attacked Zak at Fell End. Rye knew that for some reason those moments were important, but he simply could not recall them.

"You will find Farr in Riverside, Rye, I am sure," he heard Sonia say lightly. "And Sholto and Dirk, too, perhaps. You told me that the Fell End wounded were left there."

Rye's head throbbed. Sonia's voice had been too casual. She wanted to find Dirk and Sholto far more urgently than she was admitting.

Sholto in particular, no doubt, Rye thought. But he

said nothing, and in silence moved on with Sonia to the outskirts of the city and the place where the river met the sea.

Hours later, Rye was huddled in a sheltered corner of a loaded barge, weak as a baby goat and seething with frustration. His hopes of starting for Riverside without delay had come to nothing. By the time he and Sonia had reached the river docks, they had both known that he, at least, could go no farther without rest. The powers of the ring and the feather could not help him. He simply did not have the strength to run, fly, or even walk. He did not have the strength to do anything but creep into this dim hiding place with Sonia and wait for the barge to carry them upriver.

Sonia was curled up beside him, breathing evenly. Once she had helped him into shelter, she had quickly fallen asleep. Somewhere very near, a barge worker on night watch was softly playing a mouth organ. The plaintive tune drifted on the breeze, mingling with the sounds of creaking wood and lapping water.

By the light of the crystal, Rye had tried reading more of the *Three Brothers* book, but far from relaxing him, every word had made him more anxious, more desperate to be gone.

Determined to find proof that the disc in the gold casket was what he thought it to be, he had flipped through the book looking only for passages about the Fellan. He had marked those he had found by slipping shreds of straw from the barge's deck between the pages. Now he restlessly opened the book at the first of these markers and read the lines again.

✤ Since time began, the forests of Dorne have been home to beings steeped in magic. The Fellan, as they call themselves, can change their shapes at will, move from place to place in a breath, speak to one another in their minds, tame the savage beasts that share their realm, and perform many other wonders. They are beautiful to look upon, and live far beyond the normal span of human years. They do not trade or work with tools, for the forest provides them with all they need.

✤ Many of my readers know these things, I daresay. I have repeated them here for the benefit of any who do not. If the history of the Three Brothers is to be understood, the strange nature of the Fellan must be understood also.

✤ When, long ago, people from across the sea began settling on Dorne's coast, the Fellan were not troubled. Fellan have no use for the coast. The sea is their enemy. The salt in the water weakens their magic, as metal does, and the fierce sun of the shore scorches their delicate skins. Besides, the Fellan of that time knew full well that though the newcomers worked with metal they were not evil beings, but merely wanderers seeking a home.

✤ For some time, the two peoples lived in

harmony — and indeed marriages between Fellan and newcomers were not uncommon. The children of these unions loved the sea as well as the forest, and in their blood, the drive of the human and the magic of the Fellan were combined.

❖   It came to pass, however, as the years went by, that pioneer farmers began pushing inland, cutting trees to make open fields for crops and herds. If the Fellan resented what was happening, no one knew it, for they withdrew into the depths of their shrinking forests, and from that time on, they were rarely seen by human eyes. . . .

Gripped by the same feeling of unease he had felt the first time he had scanned these lines, Rye snapped the book shut and tied it up in the red scarf again. He closed his eyes and ordered himself to sleep, but still sleep would not come. Thoughts were flying around his mind like frantic birds trapped in an empty house.

Chieftain Farr was certainly in Riverside — Rye and Sonia had learned that much by listening to the workers who were lifting great barrels from cart after cart and stacking them onto the decks of the barges tied up at the docks. Most of the army had already marched upriver, it seemed, though some of the last troops, leaving late in the day, had made the journey in barges that had been fitted with slay shields.

Those barges were long gone. The barge on which Rye and Sonia were hiding had no shields, and would not leave until the danger of running into a slay attack in the inland had passed.

The delay would not have seemed so bad if Rye had been able to learn anything more of Farr's plans while he waited. But plainly none of the barge workers knew any more than he did.

None of them seemed to know anything about the pipeline either, or at least no one mentioned it. It was clearly visible on the other side of the river, a great silver tube mounted on stone pylons that held it clear of the ground. Perhaps the dock workers had grown so used to it that they barely saw it anymore.

The place where the pipe seemed to end — a humped shape rearing up on the shore — had been clearly visible, too, despite the darkness, when Rye and Sonia boarded the barge. No doubt it was a huge tank, Rye thought. He wondered fretfully why Farr had not had it built farther back, where it would not spoil the beauty of the shoreline. In Weld, such ugliness would never be allowed.

Then he smiled weakly at his own foolishness.

You are not in Weld now, Rye. . . .

No, he thought. The Warden of Weld had actually forbidden the building of Tallus's light columns on the grounds that the columns would clutter the city's tidy streets! It was hard to imagine anyone here, even Councilor Manx, valuing tidiness above a test that might save countless lives. Farr certainly would not. Farr would stop at nothing to protect his people.

Slow footsteps sounded on the deck. The mouth organ stopped.

"I'm thinking it'll be safe to cast off now, Jacko," a rough voice said. "It's half after midnight, and the danger area'll be well clear before we get there. With this load on, we won't make any speed at all."

"You're right there, Skip," another voice grumbled. "We're terrible low in the water."

Rye pressed the light crystal to the barrel in front of him. Through the misty window that appeared around his hand, he saw that the speakers were standing very close by. One was a wiry old man in a striped jersey, a mouth organ in his hand. The other was heavily built, with a closely shaven head and several gold earrings.

"Have you looked in any of these here barrels, Skip?" the old man asked. "Nothing in them but junk, that I can see. It's beyond me why Farr wants them taken upriver."

"That's up to him," his companion replied. "He knows what he's doing, don't you worry, and we'll find out what's in his head soon enough. He's making his move the day after tomorrow, they say. Stand by, then, Jacko."

"Aye, aye, Skip."

The day after tomorrow, Rye thought in relief, settling back as the footsteps paced away. *I can still get to him in time.*

Slowly his tension drained away. The bell tree

stick and the bundle containing the gold casket and the book were safe in his belt. The little bag of charms hung around his neck, beneath his shirt. Above him, the velvet sky was scattered with bright stars.

There was a hiss of steam, and a soft chugging sound began. The barge began to move. And almost before it had left the dock, Rye was asleep.

He slept deeply, for once untroubled by dreams. And so it was that when at last he woke with a start, the loud hooting of the barge ringing in his ears, he opened his eyes on bright day.

He sat up, confused and blinking. He peered through a narrow gap between two barrels, over the side of the barge.

The riverbank was slipping by. There was the pipeline, snaking along beside the road. There were fields of brilliant yellow, and green fields where plump, placid beasts grazed. There were houses, halls, shops, and paved streets all surrounding a tower that seemed to reach to the clouds. There were people, waving. And there was a broad, weathered dock, and a proud sign facing the river:

WELCOME TO
RIVERSIDE
HOME OF THE
RIVERSIDE HOG

The barge had slowed to a crawl, but to Rye's surprise and dismay, it showed no sign of stopping. In moments, it had labored past the sign and the people who had been waving on the bank had begun turning away.

Frantically feeling in the brown bag for the red feather, Rye glanced around at Sonia. Plainly she, too, had only just woken. Despite her long sleep, she still looked very tired.

"Sonia, we must get to shore — now!" Rye whispered, gripping her arm and scrambling to his feet, pulling her with him. He made sure the hood was in place, held up the feather, and thought of flying.

He knew at once that it was no good. His feet lifted only a little way from the deck before plumping down again. He gritted his teeth and tried again, but this time, there was no result at all.

"What is wrong?" he hissed. "Why does it not work? I am rested!"

"Perhaps . . . the metal in the barge," Sonia murmured.

"Then we will have to jump."

Sonia's eyes widened. She watched silently as Rye stuffed the red feather back into the bag and pulled out the sea serpent scale.

"If the metal on the barge is the problem, this will work once we are in the water," Rye told her. "We are not far from the bank."

Sonia hesitated only a moment before giving a brief nod. Together they squeezed out of their hiding place and slipped along the loaded deck to a place where the side railing was clear.

Halfway over the railing, Rye's stomach lurched. He had forgotten about the book! Water would destroy it! Frantically he began tearing at the knots that fastened the red bundle to his belt.

"Ho!" a startled voice yelled behind him. "Skip, look! Gordy, get over here! We've got a couple of stowaways! There, by the rail!"

"They can see us!" Sonia panted. "Oh, Rye —"

Feet began to pound toward them. There was a clang and a curse as someone stumbled, but a second pair of feet ran on.

The old man called Jacko appeared from behind a stack of barrels and made for them, his hands reaching out to grab them.

The bundle came free at last. Holding it high above his head, Rye tightened his grip on Sonia.

"Now!" he roared. And together they jumped with a second to spare, leaving Jacko leaning over the railing, bawling curses as he snatched at empty air.

RIVERSIDE

The river was running swiftly and its chill made Rye and Sonia gasp, but they quickly discovered that they had no need of the serpent scale. They were so close to the bank that the water was only chest deep. They could wade to safety.

And wade they did, clinging together while the tide tugged at them and pebbles slipped beneath their feet, till they reached the mossy stone bank. And then they crawled out and looked behind them.

The barge was chugging on, gradually picking up speed. Clearly the captain had no intention of stopping just to chase two ragged stowaways. Jacko was still standing at the railing, looking back in puzzlement, his hand shading his eyes.

"He cannot see us," Sonia cried gleefully. "The hood must be working again!"

Her face had brightened. The dip in the river seemed to have done her good. Rye felt far better himself, he realized. It was a relief to know that the powers had not deserted him. He simply had not realized that there was enough metal in the barge to make them useless.

He and Sonia were standing on a well-paved road not far past the township. From the barge, Riverside had looked of modest size, but from this angle, Rye could see that in fact it was very large. Bordered by checkered fields of yellow and green, it stretched back from the road in a long, narrow band as far as the eye could see. Rye could only imagine that the farmland on either side of the band was particularly rich, too valuable to be used for building.

On the other side of the road was the pipeline. It was bigger than it had seemed from a distance, and its stone supports raised it so high above the ground that even the tallest man could have walked beneath it without ducking his head.

"It is a mammoth work," Rye said, staring at it in wonder as he pushed the serpent scale back into the brown bag.

"It is monstrous," Sonia replied flatly.

As Rye glanced at her in surprise, she shrugged and turned away.

"It gives me a bad feeling. I cannot explain it," she said. "Let us go! For one thing, there will be food in Riverside and I am as hungry as a clink!"

"We have no money," Rye muttered, suddenly aware of how hollow his own stomach felt.

"Then we will have to eat scraps or steal!" Sonia retorted. She pulled at Rye's arm, and he began walking with her toward the Riverside dock. The sun was hot. Already their wet clothes had begun to steam.

"What is that yellow crop, do you suppose?" Rye asked, looking over the fields.

Sonia laughed. "Do you not know? That is myrmon!"

"*Myrmon?* But that was —"

"Yes! The stuff that Bird and her people used to put Dirk and me to sleep! But here myrmon is used to help people who are in pain — not to take them prisoner!"

She laughed again, her eyes sparkling. "Myrmon was one thing I learned about when I passed Riverside on my way to you. It is quite a new crop, bred here, and they are all very proud of it. The sleeping potion is made from the centers of the flowers, the stems make very good feed for animals, and the petals give a yellow dye that never fades. Myrmon has helped make Riverside and the surrounding farms rich! That and the famous Riverside hogs."

"A new crop, developed here!" Rye exclaimed. "And the hogs . . . Sonia, the fields around here must be rich with jell! That is why the people of Riverside have left them as farmland, instead of building on them."

142

"Then surely it will not be long before the Master invades in earnest," Sonia replied darkly. "I cannot think why he has not made his move already. You had better tell Farr that, as well as everything else."

They reached the Riverside sign, and under cover of the hood slipped into the city unnoticed. Looking around, Rye was surprised to see so few soldiers on the streets, and decided that the main army must be stationed farther away from the river.

To his surprise, he was feeling very comfortable. Riverside was a place of light, color, and space. The broad, paved roads were busy but less bustling than the crowded streets of the larger city by the sea. The brightly dressed citizens exchanged smiles and greetings as they passed one another, and when, as often happened, two or three stopped to chat, people simply moved around them with no sign of impatience.

A bakery was offering free samples of a new kind of bread, so the companions helped themselves from the basket, hoping that no one would notice the warm, crusty fragments disappearing into thin air. The bread was delicious, but they did not dare take too many pieces at once, and regretfully moved on, their stomachs growling for more.

Reaching a small square with a bubbling fountain in its center and wooden benches set around its edges, they sank into a corner to rest and look about them.

"This is a good town," Sonia said suddenly. "I feel very peaceful here."

"I was thinking the same thing," Rye agreed.

Indeed, there was something very attractive about Riverside. People were sitting all around the square, talking, reading, or simply enjoying the air. A light, cooling breeze flitted through the surrounding streets, fluttering the edges of the striped awnings that stretched from most of the buildings, providing welcome shade. Stone water troughs for animals stood here and there. And Rye was warmed to see that many of the houses and shops had been built around tall rock chimneys hollowed out by clinks long ago.

"This place must have been a clink colony once, like Fleet," he said. "Look at the chimneys!"

"I daresay they are blocked in the summer," Sonia replied drily.

Rye said nothing. He, too, had noticed that almost all the town's windows and doors were fitted with metal shields that would slide across them at sunset.

The citizens of Riverside, going so cheerfully about their business, were besieged, just as the people of Weld were. They, too, had to lie in their beds at night in stifling houses, listening to the sounds of death brushing their sealed walls.

Still, they were not suffering like the people of Weld. Only a few scattered skimmers made their way to Riverside, it seemed, compared to the hordes that descended on the city inside the Wall. And, perhaps even more importantly, the Riverside citizens plainly did not feel trapped and helpless. Their houses were sturdy and well shielded, and they knew that Farr and his council were striving to stop the menace.

The red bundle on Rye's belt seemed suddenly very heavy. He sat straighter, looking anxiously around.

"We must find out where Farr is," he said abruptly. "I must get to him before he makes his move tomorrow."

And as Sonia drew breath to answer, perhaps to say that they should find Sholto and Dirk before they did anything else, the peace of the square was shattered. A man in a soldier's uniform bolted in from the street with several other soldiers in hot pursuit.

"Stop him!" the leading soldier roared. "He tried to kill Farr! Stop him!"

Shocked, the other people in the square half rose from their seats as the running man splashed heedlessly through the little fountain, intent on escape. Without a thought, Rye jumped up and stuck out his foot.

The running man had no chance. He tripped over the invisible obstacle and fell heavily. In seconds, the soldiers were upon him. He snarled and struggled as they hauled him to his feet.

And only then did Rye realize who he was. The prisoner, the man who had tried to kill Chieftain Farr, was the scar-faced guard, Jett.

"Let me go!" Jett roared. "I am innocent!"

"Then you were a fool to run!" growled the leading soldier, holding him firmly by the arm. "Be steady now, man! If you are innocent, you have nothing to fear."

"He is not innocent, and he has everything to fear!" Councilor Manx had swept into the square, with Barron, Sigrid, and some other robed people panting behind him.

A crowd of onlookers was quickly gathering. The little square was becoming more crowded by the moment. Rye and Sonia edged quickly behind their bench to keep out of the way.

"We all saw it!" Manx cried in ringing tones. "This man brought in a food tray and put it before the chieftain. He then backed away and tried to leave the room quickly, in a way I thought suspicious. I at once inspected the tray. Beneath one of the covers was a device primed with blasting powder stolen from the pipeline workers' stores and set to explode in moments!"

Sigrid, her iron-gray braids hanging down her back and bright red patches burning high on her cheekbones, nodded vigorously.

"All this is true," she panted. "Councilor Barron most bravely seized the device and ran with it to the water closet where it was safely quenched. If it had not been for his actions, Farr would now be dead, and we, the only three of his councilors who know the plan to foil the enemy, would be dead with him."

"Lies!" Jett shouted, struggling violently.

"Not lies, you wretch!" Barron spluttered. "Truth! We all saw the device! We all saw you run!"

Manx pursed his lips and raised his chin. "Guards, take this man to the watchtower! Lock him up! He will be dealt with when Chieftain Farr —"

"When Chieftain Farr has done what he came upriver to do." The deep voice was somber. The onlookers drew back, awestruck, as the tall figure of the chieftain entered the square.

And through a gap in the moving crowd, Rye suddenly saw Dirk and Sholto standing together not far away. They were wearing unfamiliar clothes, and small red knapsacks were slung on their backs. Dirk's arm was in a sling. Sholto was leaning on a stick. They both looked ill and pale. But they were alive!

A great, burning lump rose in Rye's throat. Tears sprang into his eyes. Until that moment, he had not known how strong his secret fears for his brothers had been. He felt Sonia sway beside him as his powerful emotion crashed into her mind without warning.

Where, Rye?

There! There! They live, Sonia! Both of them!

He felt her joy and relief lapping through him like warm, fragrant water, surrounding him, then flowing on to gather Dirk and Sholto in its embrace. He saw Sholto raise his head and look around, his brow creased in puzzlement, his clever eyes scanning the crowd.

We are here, Sholto! In the corner. Behind the bench. Come!

It seemed to Rye that he and Sonia were calling with one mind, one voice. He had never felt anything

147

like it before. His whole body thrilled as he saw Sholto touch Dirk's arm, murmur to him, and begin sidling awkwardly through the crowd, toward the corner. Dirk followed, frowning and glancing repeatedly at Jett.

"Chieftain, I am not guilty!" Jett cried, holding out his arms to Farr. "Do not believe —"

"Silence, Jett!" Farr's face was seamed with gray lines. His eyes were bleak. "This is a bitter day. I have trusted you, but you have deceived me utterly. I must believe the evidence of my own eyes. The makings for the device have been discovered hidden among your possessions."

The crowd shouted angrily. Jett shrank back, showing his teeth like a cornered beast.

"I always thought it suspicious that he was so eager to guard the spy Keelin," Sigrid said tightly. "I told you so, Farr, at the beginning. Both of them injured when you took them in! Neither of them carrying proof of who they were or where they came from! Both with strange patterns of speech that proved they were foreigners! It seems my suspicions were justified. They were in league!"

Rye felt a chill. Sonia tightened her grip on his arm.

"Plainly," snapped Manx. "And the plot was a deep one. Jett has been in Farr's service for years."

"By the stars!" Barron groaned. "If only we had unmasked them before poor old Carryl . . ."

His chin wobbled, and he hurriedly pulled out a handkerchief and blew his nose loudly.

"I had nothing to do with the explosion at the museum, you bloated windbag!" Jett snarled. "I do not make war on children and old women!"

"That is enough!" Farr snapped. "Take him away!"

Again the crowd parted as the soldiers holding Jett began wrestling him none too gently out of the square. The expression on the prisoner's scarred face was desperate, ferocious. He fought like a wild man, bellowing that he was innocent of any crime. Twice he almost slipped through the hands that gripped him. Twice he was secured again. At last, the biggest of his captors twisted his arm behind his back and he screamed in pain.

"Barbarians!" he roared. "Filthy barbarians!"

Rye's stomach turned over. He looked wildly at Sholto, still moving determinedly toward them, at Dirk, who was staring in horror at the struggling man, and finally at Sonia.

Sonia had clapped her hand over her mouth. "Can it be?" she breathed through her fingers.

Rye nodded grimly. "Yes," he said. "I am sure of it, and by Dirk's face, he knows it, too. Jett is one of us. He is from Weld."

THE WATCHTOWER

As soon as Jett had been taken away, Farr and his councilors left the square. The crowd followed eagerly. Dirk and Sholto stood waiting while the chattering tide surged past them. And at last, the little square was as bare as a wave-washed shore except for the two who waited and the two standing invisible in the shelter of Rye's hood.

The shock of Jett's arrest could not overshadow the glad reunion of the four. Their relief at finding one another safe and well was so great that even Sholto could not hide his joy.

Dirk seemed to assume that Sholto had caught a glimpse of Rye and Sonia, and Sholto did not correct him. Neither did Sonia, who merely looked amused. Perhaps, Rye thought, Sholto had convinced himself that Dirk must be right, and that the call he had felt was simply his brain playing tricks. Sholto would believe anything before accepting that people could speak mind to mind.

Well, now is no time to make him uneasy by trying to persuade him differently, Rye thought. *Soon enough there will be something more important I will have to make him accept.* He touched the red bundle at his belt, feeling the shapes of the gold casket and the book, and silently warned Sonia to say nothing of them for now.

Food, at least, was no longer a problem. The red knapsacks, which had been given to Dirk and Sholto that morning on their release from the Riverside healer's care, were packed with supplies. Soon Rye and Sonia were eating ravenously, talking and listening at the same time.

Dirk and Sholto had heard that Farr was to attack the following day, but they knew very little else. There had been no talk of war in the quiet chambers guarded by the Riverside healer. The only whisper they had heard on the streets since their release was that many of the soldiers would be armed with weapons called "flamers."

"Perhaps 'flamer' is another name for 'scorch,'" Rye suggested hopefully. If Farr's troops carried the deadly weapons Olt's Gifters had wielded, they would be able to defend themselves from the Master's gray guards, at least.

Dirk shook his head. "Nothing so powerful, I fear. Flamers sound like very crude devices — heavy, and difficult to aim, from what I heard."

"It does not matter what weapons Farr's soldiers use," Sholto said restlessly. "The Master cannot be defeated by ordinary means. He commands powers that . . . that we cannot understand."

It was the closest he had ever come to admitting that the Lord of Shadows was a sorcerer. Rye knew there would never be a better time to tell his secret. Hastily he freed the red cloth bundle from his belt and unwrapped it.

Dirk and Sholto exclaimed over the casket and looked at the disc inside with interest, but to Rye's dismay, they did not seem to feel the disc's magic at all. And as he told them his plan, his words tumbling over themselves in his eagerness to explain, they both looked at him as if he had lost his senses.

"Farr will never ask the Fellan for help, Rye," Dirk said. "He knows they are not to be trusted, and you should know it, too. Have you forgotten that they stood by and let hundreds of Weld heroes die horribly in their cursed forest? By the Wall, I have not!"

"Yes, but —" Rye bit his lip. If only he could explain why he had faith in the guardians of the Fell Zone! For a moment, he considered breaking his solemn promise not to tell where the bag of powers had come from, but his throat closed at the thought. He could not do it, and Sonia was bound by the same promise.

"If the Fellan were the ones who made my mind a blank and drove me into the Saltings, I agree they are not to be trusted," Sholto said. "Also, I think you are putting too much faith in that disc, Rye. If the Fellan are as powerful as you say, how could a mere object stop them from doing anything they wished?"

Rye shook his head in frustration. "To the Fellan, the disc is not just an object! It is the symbol of an oath they cannot break. See here! I found this last night — it proves I am right!"

He flipped through the little book till he found the page he wanted, and read aloud:

✤   **The chieftain swore that the forests of the center would remain Fellan territory, forbidden to outsiders. The Fellan, in their turn, <u>swore that they would not trouble the newcomers or interfere in the wider affairs of Dorne</u>. And so the agreement was forged, for good or ill, and <u>a charm was struck to be its sign</u>.**

"You see?" Rye exclaimed. "The disc may have been lost for centuries, and Farr's people may have forgotten how the agreement began, but to the Fellan, it still stands."

He looked up to see Dirk and Sholto exchanging dubious glances and Sonia looking down at her hands.

"Farr will understand me, even if you do not!" he said angrily. "I am going to him now!"

"You will not get in to see Farr now, Rye," Dirk said, with a kindly patience that Rye, in his present mood, found infuriating. "By this time, he is again locked away with his councilors."

"And if my ears did not deceive me, Rye, you are thought to be an enemy spy," Sholto murmured. "You should keep out of sight and leave Farr to Dirk and me. We had always planned to see him as soon as he was alone. We will tell him what we know of the enemy, and with luck, he will believe us and at least postpone the attack."

Rye opened his mouth to argue, but Sonia lifted her head and spoke before he could say anything.

"I agree that Farr will never be persuaded to take the disc to the Fellan," she said coolly. "And I agree that Rye will be in danger if anyone sees him here."

"Good!" said Dirk, looking rather surprised. "So —"

"So Rye and I will return the disc to the Fellan ourselves, and see what comes of it."

Dirk was speechless. Rye shook his head. "Sonia, I told you, Farr should be the one to —"

"If Farr is unwilling, someone else must do it," Sonia broke in. "And who better than you, Rye?"

Her eyes met his. Her voice whispered in his mind.

Who better than the one the Fellan trusted with the nine powers?

"The Fellan here are not — not friendly to me," Rye stammered.

"They are Fellan, wherever they are," Sonia said quietly. "However they feel, they will recognize the truth."

Sholto was watching her intently. She returned his gaze with a defiant toss of her head.

"You cannot know it *is* the truth, Sonia!" Dirk growled. "You are relying on a tale from an old book that might be nothing but make-believe!"

"Could I see it, Rye?" Sholto asked, holding out his hand.

A little reluctantly, Rye passed over the book. Sholto began flipping through it, scanning a few sentences here and there as he had always done at home when he was deciding if something was worth reading.

"Interesting," he said after a moment, and went back to the beginning.

Dirk frowned. "I do not care how interesting it is! Rye cannot go into danger, chasing after a myth that may or may not be real!"

"It *is* real," Rye said stoutly. "And Sonia is right. If Farr is out of the question, she and I must go to the Fellan. You cannot stop us, Dirk!"

Dirk stared at him for a long moment, then grimaced. "No, I cannot stop you. Once I could have, I daresay, little brother, but those days are gone."

Ruefully he rubbed his forehead with his good hand. "Very well — have it your own way. But not before you have helped us release Jett. I doubt Sholto and I can do it alone, the way we are. We will need the hood and the key, at least."

"Surely Jett is safe enough where he is for now," Sholto objected, his eyes on the book.

"He is not," said Dirk grimly. "If Jett stays in the watchtower, he will not survive the night. Nothing is more certain."

Rye felt a thrill of horror. "But Farr would never allow —"

"Farr will have nothing to do with it. Somehow the real assassin will manage the business so that it looks as if Jett killed himself rather than face questioning. We cannot let that happen. Jett is one of our own. He has been falsely accused —"

"How can you know that?" Sonia demanded, frowning.

"Because I know him," Dirk said simply. "He was one of the Northwall volunteers. Joliffe, Crell, and I met him at the Keep. Jett was the leader of the Northwall riots. He is passionately loyal to Weld. He would never have tried to kill Farr, who is facing the same enemy as Weld and is our natural ally."

Sholto looked up, his finger marking his place. "Then the proof of his guilt must have been planted in his room."

"Yes," Dirk said grimly. "And if he dies tonight without speaking, the real spy will be safe and free to try again."

There was no more to be said. Even Sonia, who was plainly burning to be gone, could not face the thought of leaving Jett to his fate. Trusting the book to Sholto, who plainly did not want to part with it, Rye wrapped the gold casket in the scarf again and tied it back to his belt. Then he slipped the armor shell onto his little finger, and in the shelter of the hood, he and Sonia followed Dirk and Sholto to the watchtower.

The tower was only one street back from the river, and looked newer than the shops and dwellings around it. It was built of stone and taller than any building that Rye had ever seen. At the top it was lined with windows. Its base was solid, with a single iron door. The ground in front of it was neatly paved, and behind it was a little park, shaded by graceful old trees.

A few elderly people were sitting in the park, placidly watching children play. The paving outside the iron door, however, was crowded with people who were in a very different mood.

"Bring him out!" a man shouted to the soldier standing on guard by the door. "We'll show him what we think of spies and killers!"

Their faces ugly with hate, the people behind him roared and pressed forward.

The four companions drew together so that they all shared the concealment of the hood, but there was no danger. The crowd was far too intent on the door to notice what was happening anywhere else.

"We can do nothing here," Sholto said in a low voice. "Unless we wish to be discovered before we begin."

He was right, of course. Dirk, Rye, and Sonia could all see it. The way to the door was completely blocked. If they tried to fight their way through the crowd, invisible and armored, everyone would know that a rescue attempt was being made — a rescue attempt using magic, too. It would make the guard and the crowd even more convinced that Jett was an enemy assassin. The guards would kill him before they would see him go free.

"We will just have to wait until the crowd moves away," Dirk said, gritting his teeth.

We cannot wait! We must take the disc to the Fell Zone! Time is short!

Rye did not know if the thought was Sonia's or his own. He looked up. The windows at the top of the tower glinted in the sunlight.

"The door is not the only way in," he said slowly. He felt in the brown bag and pulled out the feather and the golden key.

Sholto's pale face took on a greenish tinge, but he said nothing. Dirk frowned.

"I am not sure I can fly with you, Rye," he said reluctantly, touching the sling that supported his right arm. "This arm is useless, and the burns on the other are still very painful."

"Sholto's leg is plainly not fit for crawling about tower steps either," Sonia snapped. "Rye and I will go for Jett. You two wait here and decide where he is to be hidden."

"Yes, ma'am!" Dirk replied drily.

Sonia's eyes widened, and she shrank back a little as if she had been slapped. Then she recovered and shot Dirk a scathing look.

"If you have a better plan, by all means tell us what it is," she said coldly.

As Dirk, looking a little abashed, shook his head, Rye raised the feather.

"Wait!" Sholto exclaimed. "Sonia —"

For an instant, Rye thought his brother was actually going to beg Sonia to stay in safety on the ground. Then he saw that Sholto was pressing a tiny bottle and a white cloth into Sonia's hand.

"This is extract of myrmon," Sholto said. "I — ah — borrowed it from the healer's store, thinking it might prove useful. Three drops on the cloth will put a grown man to sleep. Do not use more, or your victim may never wake."

"Thank you," Sonia said, tucking the little bottle and the rag into her pocket.

Sholto bowed. "I am sure you would do the same for me."

With very mixed feelings, Rye tightened his grip on Sonia and raised his eyes to the glinting windows. *Up,* he thought, and felt her thoughts echoing his. *Up! Up!*

There was no faltering this time. Between one heartbeat and the next, it seemed, Rye was pressing the golden key to one of the tower windows, and he and Sonia were tumbling inside.

The small square room was flooded with sunlight. It contained only a chair and a table on which lay a long metal tube with thick glass at both ends — a far glass, Rye knew, used for making distant objects look larger and closer. Tallus had one like it, though his was made of polished goat bone.

There was a trapdoor in the bare wooden floor. It was easily raised, and after that, everything went more smoothly than Rye could have hoped in his wildest dreams. The light crystal guided him and Sonia down the circular steps that led down from the trapdoor. The crystal's power showed them what was behind the locked door that at last barred their way, and the golden key opened the door with only the tiniest of clicks.

Weighed down with iron chains bolted to the wall, Jett was huddled in a cell in a corner of the room. There was only one guard, and he was sitting drowsing on a stool, facing his prisoner. Sonia's myrmon-sprinkled cloth subdued him in moments. The key opened the cell, and with only a little more trouble, the padlocks on the chains as well. Jett, who had clearly been beaten, was mumbling and half unconscious, but still able to drag himself up to the tower room with Rye and Sonia's help.

And then the trapdoor was closing behind them, and they were blinking in the sunlit room where they had begun. The whole rescue had taken no more than a few minutes.

"Rest here a moment, Jett," Rye said, pushing back the hood and leading the injured man to the chair. "Then we will take you out of here."

At the sound of his voice, Jett stirred. He licked his torn lips, and his half-closed eyes strained open. He saw Rye and gave a violent start.

"You!" he rasped. "Keelin!"

"Do not fear," Rye said quickly. "We have come to get you out. We are from Weld, as you are. We know you are not guilty. We know you did not try to kill Chieftain Farr."

A curious expression crossed Jett's battered face. His mouth strained open, and a hoarse, barking sound came out.

For an instant, Rye thought he was having some sort of fit. Then he realized his mistake. The man was laughing.

"You fool!" Jett howled. "Of course I tried to kill Farr! By the Wall, how could you doubt it? I tried to blow him off the face of Dorne, and his poisonous councilors with him! Of course I am guilty — guilty as sin!"

THE ENEMY OF WELD

It was a moment Rye would never forget — a moment of shock, confusion, horror, and pity. As Jett stood there in front of him, sweat starting out on his brow, blood seeping from his ruined mouth, Rye could not help but think that the man had lost his senses.

But it was not so. That was clear the moment Jett spoke again.

"Did you think I was a traitor like you, *Keelin*?" he sneered. "Did you think that I, too, was a groveling pet of the enemy of Weld?"

Stunned, Rye gaped at him.

"I was drawn to the golden Door, but in the old tales, it is always the humblest choice that is the right one," Jett went on, his swollen eyes glittering. "So I went through the wooden Door. I fought my way through the Fell Zone. I found the enemy of Weld. I gained a place in his household. I bided my time, waiting my chance to kill him without fear of discovery so I could return home and claim my prize. I was a fool. I should have acted at once. . . ."

He stopped to gasp for breath. With the back of his hand, he swiped at the blood trickling down his chin, smearing it across his cheek. All the time, he glared at Rye as if Sonia, standing motionless by the trapdoor, did not exist.

"How did you survive the Fell Zone without harm, *Keelin*?" he snarled. "Did Farr help you? Have you been a traitor from the start? By the Wall, if I had known what you were when I saw you playing your part in Farr's evil charade at Fell End I would have seen to it that you died where you fell. But I did not realize you were from Weld till I heard you speak, and by then you were protected and it was too late."

"It was you who put that message in my dressing gown pocket," Rye whispered, his flesh creeping. "It was you who poisoned Janna and tried to poison me."

"Poison?" Jett spat. "Do not judge me by your standards, scum! A warrior of Weld does not use poison as a weapon! A dagger to the heart was what you deserved, but the witch Petronelle was always on the watch. So I wrote the note. You should have taken the warning while you had the chance. Now I will do what I have longed to do for days!"

His hands reaching for Rye's throat, he launched himself forward and fell heavily, screaming in pain and rage as the armor shell repelled him.

"Sorcerer!" he hissed, crossing his fingers and his wrists. "So that was your pay for betraying your people! That is how the enemy of Weld has made you his creature!"

"Farr is not the enemy of —"

"Liar!" Jett shouted. "Do you think I do not know? Farr has never fooled me! I have always known the skimmers were his doing. I have always known that he was duping his people, rousing their hatred, to persuade them to make war on Weld!"

"Jett, you are wrong!" Rye burst out. "Farr is not going to make war on Weld! The enemy he is about to attack is our enemy, too — a sorcerer from across the sea, who has taken possession of another part of Dorne."

Because I caused Olt's death, he thought but did not say. Because when Olt's life ended, the ring of protection he threw around this island vanished.

He fought down his guilt and concentrated on Jett, who was sneering in disbelief.

"You must believe me, Jett," he begged. "Some call this sorcerer the Master. Others call him the Lord of Shadows. He is breeding the skimmers in a place called the Harbor. I have been there! I have seen them!"

"I daresay you have, traitor!" Jett snarled. "But you cannot trick me with your half-truths! I have always known that Farr must have a powerful ally. I have always known that the skimmers were being bred far from here! How else could Farr have kept his doting people in ignorance for so long?"

He had an answer for everything. Despairingly, Rye glanced at Sonia. To his dismay, he saw that she was looking at Jett thoughtfully, biting her lip.

Sonia! You cannot believe him! He is raving! His hatred for Farr has blinded him to the truth!

Sonia met his eyes.

Or are we the ones who have been blinded?

Her question hissed into Rye's mind like chill wind. As he shook his head helplessly, more words came to him.

Ask him about the pipeline . . .

"The pipeline, Jett . . . What do you know of that?" he made himself say.

Jett gave another hoarse, bitter laugh. "I am not so stupid that I have not guessed its true purpose, if that is what you mean! I am not an oaf who thinks 'pipeline' must always mean 'water.' "

"What — what are you saying?" Rye stammered, suddenly feeling as if he was choking.

"Do you keep up the pretense even now?" Jett made an impatient movement, pushed himself up from the floor, and slumped back onto his chair.

"I know what you know, *Keelin*," he said in a flat, exhausted voice. "I know that today at sunset more skimmers than Weld has ever seen will stream from the holds of cargo ships into the giant tank where the pipeline meets the sea. I know that those skimmers will surge through the pipeline, unseen and without troubling a soul in New Nerra or Riverside. I know they will explode into the Fell Zone and fly on, over the Wall. And I know that tonight Weld will end, and that when Farr's barbarians enter it tomorrow morning, there will hardly be a soul left alive to defend it."

His head flopped forward till his chin touched his chest. He shuddered all over, then was still, as if he had suddenly fallen asleep or fainted.

And as Rye struggled against the ghastly pictures the man's words had conjured up, a memory came to him on a wave of sickness.

He saw himself standing in front of a red wall, reading a large sign:

EXTREME DANGER!
DISPATCH AREA

He saw himself creeping through a vast vault of sleeping skimmers. He saw himself pressing the light crystal to the strange, round, black-rimmed door in the back wall of the vault, and staring out at an oily, heaving sea.

And he saw the ships that waited at anchor there, each with a black circle marked low on its side — a circle to which a tunnel could be attached.

Rye! You did not tell me this! You did not mention ships waiting outside the Harbor building!

Rye's head jerked up as Sonia's voice rang in his mind. Sonia had shared his vivid memories and had drawn her own conclusions. He could feel her panic.

"Why did you not tell me, Rye?" she asked aloud. Her voice was shaking.

Rye searched for an answer. "It — was a detail. It did not seem important."

How feeble the words sounded, in the face of the fearful images flying unguarded from Sonia's mind to his! Weld facing a skimmer onslaught too great for it to bear. Annocki and Faene huddled in the damaged Keep, trying to comfort terrified, injured children while ravenous skimmers ripped and tore at the gradually crumbling walls. The Warden fluttering uselessly, never considering for a moment the idea of throwing open his private door and ushering everyone he could find down to the Chamber of the Doors, and safety.

Rye wet his lips. "Jett is only guessing," he said, hardly recognizing the sound of his own voice. "What he says cannot be true!"

"It can," said Sonia flatly. "If Sholto was here, he would tell you the same. We wondered why the Master has not invaded this place. Now we know. He does not need to invade. He and Farr are working together. Farr sends the Master Riverside hogs to work in the Diggings, food for the workers in the Harbor, myrmon for the Harbor healers. The Master sends Farr skimmers, and the means to conquer Weld."

"No!" Rye shook his head violently. "Farr is — a good man, and a great leader. He would never ally himself with the Master!"

"Farr may not know what the Master is," Sonia said, her voice hard. "He may think he can control him. He will learn better, I imagine, when at last the Master's own territory is empty of jell."

She moved to the open window, leaned on the sill, and looked out. "There is jell in plenty in those fields, we are fairly sure of that. And according to Dirk, the earth of Weld is full of it. The Master will not be able to resist mining such rich sources for long — even for the sake of hogs and myrmon."

His mind reeling, Rye joined her at the window and looked out at the countryside spread out below him like an embroidered quilt. From this great height, it seemed strangely unreal and at the same time familiar, like a place he had once seen in a dream.

He stared out at the checkered green and gold of the fields, at the gently rolling hills beyond, at the pipeline and the river with the road running in between. The Fell Zone seemed to float on the horizon like a dense green cloud. The sky above its highest point was stained an ugly brown.

Rye narrowed his eyes and bent forward, peering at the brown smudge. Was that — could it be . . . ?

He turned and snatched up the far glass from

the table. Pressing it to his eye, he focused on the brown patch of sky, then slowly lowered the glass a fraction.

And there, directly below the sickly brown haze, was the steep, bare rock of the hollow mountaintop. The stain in the sky was the exhausted breath of Weld. Rye's stomach turned over. Abruptly he took the glass from his eye, and realized that Sonia was looking at him enquiringly.

"Weld," he mumbled. "You can see it from here."

Her mouth tightened as she nodded.

Fearful of what she might go on to say, Rye made a show of looking down, as if searching for Dirk and Sholto. There were more people pressed together at the base of the watchtower now, and the number of soldiers guarding the iron door had increased to five.

The little park behind the watchtower was deserted. The old people and the children had left, no doubt because of the growing noisiness of the crowd. The park was bathed in sunlight and bright with flowers. Right in the middle, encircled by a low, clipped hedge, a small tree spread its graceful branches over a large stone tablet that perhaps bore the park's name, or a list of the founders of Riverside.

Rye's eyes blurred as he looked down at the green patch of peace. The tree could easily be a bell tree. Almost he could imagine that he was looking down at the garden in the Fleet guesthouse, where Sonia and Faene had walked not so long ago, their hair loose and shining in the sun, their light dresses floating in the gentle breeze.

That garden had been a place of peace, too. Until Olt's Gifters came.

I cannot regret causing Olt's death, Rye thought suddenly. *I cannot! But I can try to stop the evil that flowed from it. And by chance I have the means.*

He touched the bundle hanging from his belt. It was less bulky now, because Sholto had the book, but the gold casket was safe.

"If Farr is in league with the Master, or if he is not, does not matter," he said aloud. "We will take the disc to the Fellan as we planned."

"Time is short," Sonia murmured. She was still staring out the window, staring at the horizon. At Fell End, where the pipeline ended? At the forbidden forest? At the murky cloud that marked Weld? Rye could not tell.

As he looked with her, a tiny flash caught his eye. On the road beyond the hills, something was winking like a tiny beacon. He lifted the far glass.

Six people on horseback were moving toward Fell End. The leader had a short, broad sword in his belt, and it was this that was catching the light. He sat tall in the saddle, and was bareheaded.

It was Farr. Rye knew it. The three councilors were riding behind him, and behind them were two soldiers. Their shadows were long and dark, flickering along the road like spirits bearing them company.

Rye's heart seemed to stop. Suddenly it was as if a spell had been broken — a spell that had held him for too long in this small square room where everything could be seen distantly, from above.

If Jett was right, sunset would mean the end of Weld.

A plan sprang into Rye's mind, fully formed. He dug his fingers into the brown bag, searching for the charms he needed. "We must go!" he exclaimed.

Sonia turned sharply, her eyes startled.

Rye clambered onto the windowsill, pulling her with him. "Farr has left Riverside," he panted, holding up the red feather. "It looks as if he is on his way to — to Fell End!"

"Rye, wait!" Sonia gasped. "You have not —"

"Jett can stay where he is," Rye muttered, and flung them both into space. He felt the breeze from the river cool on his hot face, his neck, his ears. Only then did he realize what Sonia had been trying to tell him. He was not wearing the hood. He had forgotten to pull on the hood!

There was a crash behind them as Jett's chair fell to the floor. Then Jett himself was at the window, bawling to the crowd below, stabbing his finger at Rye and Sonia.

"Sorcerers!" Jett roared as shocked faces turned upward and people began to scream, crossing their fingers and their wrists at the sight of two beings swooping like birds above them. "You see? I am innocent! There are your assassins! Do not let them get away!"

171

UPSTREAM

In seconds, arrows were flying into the air. The soldiers' aim was deadly. If it had not been for the armor shell, Rye and Sonia would have perished at once. As it was, the arrows simply bounced away from them. The crowd cried out in terror and disbelief. The soldiers cursed, fitted fresh arrows to their bows, and tried again, just as uselessly.

Rye struggled to pull on the hood, but it was flapping behind him in the wind and the silk kept slipping through his fingers. Desperately he scanned the ground, and at last caught sight of Dirk and Sholto edging back toward the little park, their shocked faces upturned.

What a fool they must think me, Rye told himself. *How could I have forgotten the hood?* He felt the power of the feather waver and heard Sonia catch her breath.

Grimly he thrust his shame aside and focused his mind on his brothers, on reaching his brothers. . . .

"No!" Sonia cried, hearing his thoughts. "Leave them, Rye! They are safe here. No one saw them with us. And neither of them is fit to fly!"

Rye shut his mind to her. His faith in Farr had been badly shaken, but part of him still could not believe the man was his enemy. In Fell End, he would find out for sure, and whatever happened after that, he wanted Dirk and Sholto with him.

He swooped downward, shouting to Dirk and Sholto to be ready. His eyes stung and watered as the air beat into his face. The ground came rushing up to meet him — a blur of green, a blur of stone, his brothers' faces, their mouths gaping. And then he was off the ground again, with Dirk and Sholto clinging to him, and was hurtling above the heads of the crowd through a hail of stones and arrows.

"Rye, this is madness!" Sholto roared. "Dirk cannot —"

"Hold on to him," Rye roared back. "Just a few more seconds . . ."

They were soaring over the pipeline, skimming over the road. And there was the river, its rippling surface gleaming in the sun.

As they flew over the bank, Rye pushed the red feather deep into his pocket and pulled out the sea serpent scale he had put there in readiness. An instant later, his companions were yelling in shock as they all plowed into the river. Cool water opened to receive them, rose to cover them as they sank.

With elation, Rye felt the pain in the palm of his hand that told him the serpent scale had sunk into his flesh. Strength flowed through him. Effortlessly he twisted in the water and slid beneath Sonia till in her panic she caught hold of his shoulders. He wrapped one arm around Dirk, the other around Sholto. Then he shot to the surface, dragging them all with him.

"Swim!" he ordered. "Feel what you can do!"

He barely heard the bellows of shock from the riverbank as he surged forward, carving through the water as if it were air, leaving a trail of foam behind him. His companions were no weight at all, and soon they were all helping him, feeling what he felt, reveling in their mastery of the current that pushed vainly against them.

It did not matter that Rye could not use his arms, or that Dirk and Sholto were injured. By the power of the enchanted scale, they all streaked through the water like serpents, more often below the surface than above, leaving their pursuers far behind.

So they passed through low hills without seeing them, passed fields of green and gold without knowing it, passed Farr and his companions who turned in their saddles to stare. And in what seemed the blink of an eye, the Fell End jetty was beside them, and they were gliding to a stop behind a half-unloaded barge.

No one in Fell End had seen them arrive. People were working far too feverishly on land to notice a disturbance in the river. Rye pulled the hood of concealment over his head, and the companions peered over the flat deck of the barge.

The Fell End riverbank looked very different from the way it had when they had first seen it. Then, the bank had been green and peaceful, a welcome banner had fluttered over the jetty and music had filled the air. Now the riverbank was churned mud, and crowded with barrels that were being rolled and hefted onto carts. Hundreds of loaded carts already stood in lines along the metal barrier that separated the town from the Fell Zone. Soldiers were laboring side by side with pipeline workers. People not strong enough to work with the barrels were scurrying around with drinking water for those who were. It seemed that every soul in the town was on the riverbank, engaged in this one mighty task.

And above them the pipeline soared, complete. Clutching the side of the barge, looking up, Rye felt his mouth go dry. The vast silver pipe continued almost all the way to the metal barrier, then tilted steeply upward, so it looked like the neck of a giant sea serpent rising high above the waves. It even straightened at the top, stretching over the fence like the serpent's head.

But the "serpent's" gaping mouth was rimmed in black. And sealed to the black rim was a great length of broad, clear tube. The tube was not rigid like the pipeline. It dangled from the black circle like a snake the "serpent" was swallowing, trailing down to coil on the Fell End side of the barrier. It was so enormously long that the coils formed a mound as large as the chieftain's lodge in the city by the sea.

Sonia, Dirk, and Sholto were staring, aghast. Like Rye, they had seen tubing like that before. They had seen it, in miniature, attached to skimmer cages in the testing hall of the Master. They had seen skimmers hurtle through it and burst out into the air in a frenzy to feed.

"What does this mean?" Dirk whispered.

Rye swallowed, struggling to find an answer that would allow him to keep his faith in Farr. "It may not mean anything. New Nerra is a trading port. Goods come to it from all over the Sea of Serpents."

"Oltan is a trading port, too," Dirk muttered. "Yet there is nothing like that soft, clear pipe there. I have only ever seen it in one other place before."

"That piping, and the black seal, are the Master's work," Sholto said evenly. "Farr could not have obtained them from anyone else."

Rye could not speak. It was left to Sonia to tell what Jett had said in the watchtower. When she had finished, there was silence. Dirk and Sholto were both staring in horror at the rearing pipeline and at the great mound of tubing that, uncoiled and stretched to its full length, would surely reach all the way up through the Fell Zone, to Weld.

"So now we know why the soldiers are armed with flamers," Dirk said heavily at last. "They are going to burn a track through the forest, to make way for the people dragging the tube."

Sholto's face was haggard. "And they will be beginning that task very soon, no doubt. They have left it till the last minute, but, after all, the skimmers cannot be released before sunset."

In dread, Rye looked up at the dimming sky.

"Rye," Sonia whispered, clutching his cold hand. "We must go to the Fellan — all of us! The disc is our only chance! You know now that there is no point in trying to talk to Farr."

And at that moment, with a great flurry of hooves, Farr himself rode in, with his windblown councilors and guards trailing behind. A few men and women hurried to greet him.

"Where are they?" Farr thundered, leaping from his horse and drawing his sword.

"Who, sir?" one of the men asked in confusion.

"Copper-heads!" Farr shouted. "Four of them! Swimming upriver like a shoal of serpents! We saw them from the road. They passed us! They are here — they must be here! Look alert!"

Copper-heads. As the soldiers on the riverbank scattered, Rye turned to Sonia. She stared back at him, her eyes wide and dark, her drying hair tumbling about her shoulders, a mass of coppery red. The river had washed away the brown dye.

Rye knew the same thing must have happened to him. He raised his hand to his head. The last of the bandage was gone, too, stripped away by the current. At last he understood why Petronelle had insisted he keep the bandage on. Bathing his wound while he was unconscious, she had washed away some of the dye — seen the real color of his hair. She had kept her discovery to herself to protect him.

"They fear red hair," Sonia murmured, picking up his thoughts. "It reminds them of the Fellan, no doubt. Yet in Fleet red hair was not frowned upon. Faene told me she envied my hair — except that it was dangerous, because Olt prized copper-heads so highly. How could two places on the same island be so different?"

"If the people who came here were fleeing from Olt and his sorcery it is not so strange," Dirk said. "No doubt they had learned to fear all magic. And Olt and his brothers were said to be half Fellan."

"Half Fellan?" Sholto asked sharply. "Did they have red hair?"

"I cannot tell you." Dirk grimaced. "Olt was so ancient when we saw him that he had no hair whatever. Why?"

"It does not matter," Sholto muttered. But Rye could see in his face that it did matter. And suddenly he knew the reason.

"It is the book!" he exclaimed. "*The Three Brothers*! You read it, Sholto, and —"

"I read some of it," Sholto said uneasily. "It tells the story of three sorcerer brothers, half Fellan, with red hair . . . but what of it? It could be simply coincidence."

The riverbank was thick with people hunting for intruders. Farr and his councilors were standing beside the end of the barge, scanning the river. A whole troop of soldiers had drawn their weapons and run to surround the giant mound of tubing as if to guard it from attack.

"Do not move," Sholto warned softly. "They will see the ripples."

"But we *must* move!" Sonia hissed. "We must get to the Fellan before —"

"Then it is simple," Dirk cut in. "I am not fit to fly so I will stay here. You three use the feather to get yourselves out of the water and into the Fell Zone."

"Farr and his people will see where we have come from," Rye protested. "They will find you, Dirk!"

"Dirk will not be alone," Sholto said calmly. "I will stay, too. I doubt I would be of much help in the forest, but here I might be useful."

Racked with doubts, Rye clutched the edge of the barge, staring across the rough deck at the seething riverbank.

Dimly he saw that two plainly dressed women were edging out of the crowd and making their way to Farr. One of the women was sturdy, with fluffy white hair. The other was taller, younger. A drab shawl hid her hair and partly concealed her face, but to Rye, her straight back and springy walk were unmistakable.

"Janna!" Farr's face was a mask of shock. He took his wife in his arms and scowled over her head at her companion. "What do you mean by bringing her here, Petronelle!"

Janna pushed herself away from him. "Do not blame Petronelle! I told her I would make the journey with her or without her. I had to come, Farr! I am quite recovered, Zak is safe with your parents, and —"

"How could you do this, Janna?" Farr barked, but as his wife's eyes widened with startled hurt, he sighed and reached for her hand.

"I'm sorry, dear heart. But you shouldn't have come. It's dangerous — oh, in so many ways! Didn't you hear what I said? There are copper-heads here — hidden somewhere near. They may try to abduct you, use you as a tool against me."

He glanced at the sky. "It's too late to send you away now. I'll call some men to escort you and Petronelle to a shielded hut. Lock yourselves in. I'll join you when I can."

"Listen to your husband, Lady Janna," Councilor Manx said coldly as Janna drew breath to speak. "By now the enemy is aware that an attack is under way. They do not know what form the attack will take, but they fear it, and will do anything they can to stop it."

He paused, then went on deliberately. "For example, you will not have heard, I know, but today the man Jett tried to kill the chieftain — and Sigrid, Barron, and me with him."

He watched with satisfaction as Janna gasped in horror.

Farr shrugged. "It's all right, Janna. There was no harm done — except to my pride. It seems I was as wrong about Jett as I was about Keelin."

"I do not believe Keelin was an enemy," Janna murmured. "Neither does Petronelle."

"Indeed?" Manx sneered.

Janna ignored him. She looked only at her husband. "I will do as you ask, Farr, but not before I have said what I came here to say. Please, I beg you, do not go ahead with this attack. It is wrong — I feel it in my bones."

Farr gritted his teeth. "It's too late, Janna," he said harshly. "I've struggled with this decision, but now it's made I won't turn from it."

Watching intently, Rye caught his breath. If this was acting, Farr was the best actor he had ever seen. The man's face was anguished.

"The council, too, is agreed." Councilor Sigrid stepped forward with a crisp swish of skirts.

"The council has always wanted this," Janna snapped back. "But the final decision is Farr's. He is the elected chieftain."

Sigrid lifted her chin. Angry scarlet stained her high, sharp cheekbones. "The council, too, was elected by the people, Lady Janna. You were not!"

"Now then, Sigrid!" Barron chattered nervously, glancing at Farr's rigid face. "Surely Janna has a right to try to influence her husband as she sees fit?"

Sigrid turned on her heel and stalked away. With an icy glare, Councilor Manx followed her.

"Sorry, Farr," Barron mumbled. "I seem to have put my foot in it again. But I don't like it when they say your wife and the old nurse lead you by the nose."

Farr pressed his lips together, clearly biting back an irritated retort.

"Never mind," he said curtly. "Manx and Sigrid will soon discover that I make my own decisions. Just as our enemies will learn that I can't be frightened into sparing them. On the contrary, their attacks on me and those I love have made me even more determined to do what must be done."

"He is not pretending," Rye said slowly. "Jett was wrong about that, at least. Farr truly believes that Weld is his enemy. We must tell him it is not true. We must tell him —"

Dirk shook his head. "He will not listen to us, Rye."

Rye set his lips. "I will make him listen! Sholto, give me the book."

"The —" Sholto gaped at him. "Rye, the book will be nothing but pulp by now!"

"Give it to me anyway," Rye said, and taking the sodden mass Sholto passed to him, he pushed it inside his shirt.

"What are you planning, little brother?" Dirk growled suspiciously.

"In a minute, every eye will be on Farr," Rye said, pushing the loosened serpent scale into the bag of charms and digging the draggled red feather from his pocket. "That will be your chance to get out of the river and lose yourselves in the crowd. Many of the workers are almost as wet as you are. You will not be noticed. If things go wrong, get to Janna and tell her who you are. She will help you."

"And what of Sonia?" Sholto murmured.

"I will be with Rye, of course," Sonia said without hesitation.

Of course. Warmth flooded Rye's mind.

"Rye —" Dirk began.

"There is no time," Rye said, shaking and blowing on the feather in an effort to dry it. "Keep safe."

He did not have to say anything to Sonia. She had shared his thoughts and knew his plan as well as he did. Already she had taken off the faded cord she wore around her waist and was holding it in readiness. If she had any doubts about the plan's wisdom, she was keeping them to herself. He felt nothing from her but that same steady warmth.

Quietly they hauled themselves onto the damp, splintery deck of the barge. Silently they crept toward Farr. And when they were close enough, but not too close, Rye pushed back the hood.

THE HEAD OF THE SERPENT

Rye heard Councilor Barron bellow and Janna give a piercing scream. He saw Farr's head jerk around, Farr's eyes blaze at the sight of two copper-heads standing shoulder to shoulder on the barge, only paces away. He saw Farr thrust his wife behind him, into Barron's arms, and raise his sword.

Then Farr looked into Rye's face, and knew him.

"Keelin!" The rage in that one word seared Rye like a gale of flame. He stood firm. He made himself smile mockingly.

It was enough. Farr leaped onto the barge, snarling, a huge, terrifying figure. The sword slashed down with enormous force, hitting the shield thrown up by the armor shell, rebounding with a shuddering clang. And the big man was off balance, staggering. . . .

Now!

Sonia's cord whipped out like a snake and tangled around Farr's ankles. He yelled and crashed onto the deck. The next instant, Rye and Sonia were both upon him. As they thrust their arms through his heavy belt, Rye heard Janna screaming. He heard the crowd roar in dismay, and Barron squeal like a hog. And over all he heard Petronelle's despairing cry, harsh as the screech of a stalker bird.

"You swore to me, Keelin! Ah, you swore you would not harm . . ."

Up! Up! Up!

A blast of air sealed Rye's eyes and snatched the breath from his lungs. And the next moment, the shouts and screams had faded, and wind was blowing around him, tossing his hair and cooling his face.

He forced his eyes open. He, Sonia, and Farr were high above the ground. They were on the topmost point of the pipeline — perched on the head of the serpent. The giant trees of the Fell Zone rose in front of them, and directly below them were the great coils of clear tube piled against the barrier fence. They were where Rye had intended, but he had no idea how it had happened so fast.

"Well, that was all very satisfactory," Sonia murmured. "So now we beg Chieftain Farr's pardon and make him listen to us, is that it?"

"Yes," said Rye. "And we stay here for as long as it takes. Nothing will happen while Farr is thought to be in danger, and no one will dare approach us up here, for fear we will let him fall."

He turned to their silent captive. "We have done this only because we had to, Chieftain Farr," he began. "We had to talk to you. Our people are not your enemies — our people do not even know that you exist! You have been deceived! Your enemy is not who you think . . ."

His voice trailed off. It had suddenly become plain to him that Farr was not listening. The man was utterly still, staring straight ahead. Not a muscle in his face or body moved. The wind was ruffling his hair, but otherwise he might have been carved out of stone.

"Something is the matter!" Rye exclaimed. "He cannot hear me."

"He is pretending," Sonia retorted. "Or else —" She peered into Farr's motionless face and bit her lip. "Or else he is more closely linked to the Master than we thought. Remember what happened to Brand when he failed the Master at the Harbor!"

Rye nodded, his stomach heaving. But Brand had been killed. Farr was not dead, or even unconscious. He was simply — frozen.

"What now?" Sonia demanded.

Rye heard a change in the sound floating from below, and looked down quickly. The pursuing soldiers from Riverside were pounding toward the jetty, their horses' sides gleaming with sweat. People were scattering before them, shouting to them, pointing up at Rye, Sonia, and Farr.

As the soldiers reined in their horses, Rye saw with a jolt that Jett was among them. Jett's tale had been believed. He had been released from the watchtower and allowed to join the pursuit.

Well, if he came here planning to kill Farr after all, he knows now that he cannot, Rye thought grimly. Farr is out of his reach. And then, in disbelief, he saw Jett free his feet from the stirrups, stand upright on his saddle, and jump for the pipeline, his arms held high.

Jett caught hold of the pipe and swung himself up onto its curved silver surface. For an instant, he crouched motionless. Then he scrambled to his feet and, balancing like an acrobat, began walking toward the place where the pipe began to slope upward.

Jett is a master Wall worker, Rye reminded himself numbly. *Dirk could have done the same, before his arms were hurt.*

And Jett had no fear of causing Farr's death. Jett wanted Farr to die. The people below did not know that. No doubt they thought Jett was being foolishly heroic — bravely trying to save their chieftain without thinking of the danger.

Rye tore his eyes from the rapidly advancing figure and looked down at the sea of faces below. He saw Janna and Petronelle, clinging together. He saw Barron wringing his hands. . . .

Then he glimpsed Dirk and Sholto on the fringes of the crowd. Sholto was gripping Dirk's shoulder for support. Dirk was holding something loosely in his good hand. It looked like a skimmer hook.

I am dreaming, Rye thought dazedly. He blinked, and when he looked again, the crowd had shifted and his brothers were no longer in sight.

Rye, Jett is still coming!

Rye turned his eyes back to the pipeline. Jett was on his stomach, creeping up the steep slope like a caterpillar crawling up a branch. He looked up, saw Rye watching him, and grinned, showing his bloody gums and broken teeth.

"Go back, Jett," Rye heard himself call. He glanced at Farr, but Farr was still rigid, staring straight ahead, apparently seeing nothing, hearing nothing.

Jett paused, clinging to the pipe, the wind whipping his tangled hair. Sweat was streaming down his face, making runnels in the dirt and dried blood.

"Back?" he snarled. "Oh no, *Keelin*! I have worked too hard for this, planned too long, suffered too much. I am going to kill the enemy of Weld!"

He began climbing again.

"He is mad," Sonia hissed. "He knows he cannot touch us!"

"He may not know he cannot touch Farr," Rye muttered back. "Or he may not want to believe it."

But I have to make him believe it, he thought. *If he tries to attack us, he will surely overbalance and fall to his death. And Jett is a man of Weld. He is a Wall worker, like Dirk, Joliffe, and Crell. He is someone's brother, someone's son.*

"You felt our power in the watchtower, Jett!" he roared. "You cannot kill Farr while we protect him." As he spoke, he suddenly realized that he could not see Jett as clearly as he had before. He glanced up. The sky was orange, streaked with gray clouds. The sun was going down.

"The light is going!" he shouted. "Go back, Jett, before you fall!"

"I will not fall." Again Jett looked up and grinned. "And you cannot make me fear sunset either, so do not try! I know as well as you do that there will be no skimmers abroad tonight. Tonight they were to be sent through the pipeline, and all that has been stopped. Ha! How Farr must be cursing you for losing your nerve and trying to escape!"

He had almost reached the head of the serpent now. The only sounds were his laboring breaths, the scraping of his boots on the pipe, and the moaning of the wind. The shouts and cries from below had ceased. When Rye glanced down, all he could see was a mass of upturned, spellbound faces.

"We must get away from here, Rye," he heard Sonia say urgently. "We must take Farr into the Fell Zone, where Jett cannot follow."

It was the last thing Rye wanted. If Farr woke from his strange trance and found himself in the forbidden forest, he would be certain that his captors were enemies. So would Janna, Petronelle, the three councilors, and every other soul in Fell End except Dirk and Sholto.

"So, it ends at last, Chieftain Farr!"

Jett's voice was suddenly much louder. Rye's heart gave a great thud, and his head jerked up. More quickly than he had thought possible, Jett had finished his climb. Jett had hauled himself onto the flat section of pipe and was crouching there, panting, right in front of them.

The man was glaring at Farr, his eyes glittering, and at that moment, Rye saw that Sonia had been right. Jett had lost touch with reality. His mind was fixed on one simple idea — the idea that had obsessed him for so long. Kill Farr.

"Why do you stare like a dolt, Farr?" Jett sneered. "Have these traitors bewitched you? Or is it that you are shocked, great Farr, at being way up here, trussed up like a duck ready for the pot? Why, the cord is not even tied! You could kick it away easily, if you had the courage to move!"

The cord! For the first time, Rye noticed that Sonia's cord belt was still tangled around Farr's ankles.

See if you can distract Jett while I get the cord! he called to Sonia in his mind. *I will try to throw it around him — take him by surprise — and pull him close without the danger of a struggle. Then he can share the power of the feather and will be safe, whatever happens.*

Rye, you are dreaming! The cord will never hold him. He is mad, and he is very strong. We must leave him and flee into the Fell Zone. Now!

Sonia's voice had an edge to it that Rye could not quite understand. It seemed almost like fear, yet why should Sonia be fearful?

If we fly he will leap after us, Sonia. He will fall! He will die!

The answer came instantly.

Then that will be his choice. We must go. We are not safe here. I feel it!

And now Rye could feel it, too — or perhaps Sonia was at last letting fear flow from her mind into his.

Yet still he hesitated, while Jett jeered and Farr stared. He turned his head to look at the darkening trees of the Fell Zone. And so it was that he saw, rising above the distant treetops, a vast cloud of ragged, flapping wings hideously silhouetted against the gray sky.

"But —" Stupidly, Rye looked down at the pipeline. It was the same as ever. Nothing about it had changed. The clear tubing still hung slack beneath it, coiling beside the barrier fence.

Jett screamed. It was a shrill, cracked sound, as if something within him had broken.

"No!" he shrieked, staring wildly at the swelling stain in the sky. "The skimmers were to come through the pipeline tonight, from the coast into Weld. That was the plan — I worked it all out! That *must* have been the plan! Farr is the enemy of Weld! I have always known it was Farr! It *must* be Farr!"

"Plainly it is not," Rye said through stiff lips. "The skimmers are coming out of the Fell Zone, Jett! The nest is there. For Farr, the Fellan are the enemy. He has been planning to attack the Fellan, not the people of Weld. Almost certainly, he has no idea there is a city inside the Fell Zone peak."

He wondered to hear his voice sounding so calm, so level. His mind was a seething confusion of shock, horror, and a sudden, sour understanding of how ruthlessly he had been deceived and betrayed.

If skimmers roosted in the Fell Zone shade, it was because the guardians of the forest had permitted it. And that could mean only one thing: Farr was not in league with the Master, but the Fellan were.

Words Rye had read in the book now lying soaked and ruined inside his shirt flashed into his mind.

✣   It came to pass, however, as the years went by, that pioneer farmers began pushing inland, cutting trees to make open fields for crops and herds. If the Fellan resented what was happening, no one knew it, for they withdrew into the depths of their shrinking forests …

Of course the Fellan had resented the carving away of their forest home, little by little! Of course they had come to hate the impudent newcomers who had put fields and houses where trees had been before. And the city built by the Sorcerer Dann in the very center of what remained must have been — must still be — an irritation beyond bearing. To the Fellan, Weld must seem like an ugly sore in the heart of their shrunken domain. But the hollow mountaintop had become human territory as surely as the coast had, and they could not touch it.

Rye looked down at the red bundle hanging from his belt. As he thought of the shining disc, the sign of the treaty that had at last been made, more lines from the book swam before his eyes.

✣ **The chieftain swore that the forests of the center would remain Fellan territory, forbidden to outsiders. The Fellan, in their turn, swore that they would not trouble the newcomers, or interfere in the wider affairs of Dorne. And so the agreement was forged, for good or ill . . .**

How the Fellan must have regretted that treaty as time went on! But they were bound to it. So they had found a way around it.

You must make haste . . . it is almost Midsummer Eve.

"It took the Fellan a thousand years to find a way to be rid of us," Rye said aloud. "But at last a plan was made. And they used me to carry it out. They wanted Olt to die so that the Lord of Shadows could invade and clear their territory for them."

"That cannot be true," Sonia said faintly. "The Master is evil. He is destroying the land. The Fellan would never allow —"

"The Fellan care only for the center — the book says so." Rye clenched his fists as the words came back to him. How could he have read them and not realized how important they were?

Fellan have no use for the coast. The sea is their enemy. The salt in the water weakens their magic, as metal does ...

Rye's head felt as if it might burst. He could feel the bag of powers warm and pulsing against his skin like a live thing with a heart.

Nine powers to aid you in your quest ...

Powers to help the dupe of the Fellan do what the Fellan themselves could not — end Olt's life and open the way to the Lord of Shadows.

Shuddering with revulsion, Rye tore the bag from his neck so violently that the knotted drawstring snapped and pulled completely out of its casing. Its neck ragged and gaping, the bag lay in his hand like flabby skin shed by some loathsome, creeping animal. More than anything in the world he wanted to cast it away from him, see the charms scatter in the wind and be lost.

No, Rye!

Sonia's cry shrilled in Rye's mind, cutting through his rage and pain, recalling him to himself. However he felt about the powers, it would be madness to discard them now. Hastily he wound the broken string around the neck of the bag and thrust the whole untidy mess at Sonia.

"You take it, then," he muttered. "I cannot bear it near me any longer."

Sonia took the bag in silence and slid it into her pocket. Her eyes were fixed on the rising skimmers.

Like a swarm of monstrous bees, the skimmers soared upward. They wheeled as one creature. Then they dived, and even from this distance it seemed to Rye that he could see their needle teeth bared and glinting. His heart ached for Weld.

And then, directly below the diving swarm, the sky seemed to blaze. Abruptly the swarm broke into thousands of separate twisting, flapping parts as the skimmers faltered, scattered, frantic to escape the blinding flare of light.

The people defied the Warden!

"Tallus's theory was right!" Rye yelled as Sonia's astonished cry filled his mind, for an instant banishing the bitter shadows. "The light —"

But that was all he could say. His next words caught in his throat. For as he watched, the skimmer swarm was re-forming. For a moment, it swirled and eddied in the sky like a great puddle of oily water. Then it wheeled and came hurtling toward Fell End.

MAGIC

Rye's first thought was for Dirk and Sholto, and in terror, he looked down, tensing himself to fly to his brothers' aid. But the riverbank was deserted. There was nothing to be seen but churned mud, loaded carts, and dark rows of barrels. *Of course,* Rye told himself dazedly. *Everyone would have sought shelter long ago. They all know that skimmers take flight after sunset.*

And they all know where the skimmers come from, his thoughts ran on. They must have seen the swarm rising from the forbidden forest often, when the attacks first began.

For years, they had been tormented by the creatures they called slays. For years, the stragglers of the swarm had swooped on Fell End, ravaged the fields and herds of the inland, and destroyed the peace of summer nights in Riverside.

But never had the people outside the Wall felt an attack like the one there would be tonight. Tonight, repelled from their usual feeding bowl, the whole hungry skimmer swarm would fall upon the larger hunting ground that only a few hundred strays had tried before.

Rye tried to pull himself together. He knew perfectly well that the shock of having all his beliefs overturned had numbed him to his own danger, and to the danger of his companions. The sky over the Fell Zone was black with skimmers. The swarm was like a broad, wavering spear, aiming directly at the warm human flesh the skimmers could sense clinging to the highest point of the pipeline in Fell End.

Jett had stopped screaming. He was staring, his face shiny with sweat, as certain death flew toward him.

"Jett, give me your hand," Rye shouted, reaching out. "I can protect you!"

Jett shook his head violently, showing the whites of his eyes and crossing his fingers and his wrists. Grinding his teeth, Rye reached forward and seized the edge of the man's jacket. Jett quaked and moaned but did not try to pull away.

The Fell Zone, Rye! Safe there. Safe . . .

Too late . . .

Too late to fly. Too late to escape. Rye's heart sank as he remembered the skimmer attack at the Harbor, the violent battering as the creatures dashed themselves

197

senselessly at the invisible shield thrown up by the armor shell. How long could he hold on to Sonia, Jett, and Farr under that relentless buffeting? Farr would not be able to help himself. He was plainly under some sort of enchantment. But if he was not a servant of the Master, how could that be?

The swarm was almost upon them. The rasping of leathery wings filled Rye's ears. In fascinated horror, he saw the pale eyes, the flaring ears and snarling snouts of the leaders, saw the needle teeth, the great spurs curving, ready to strike.

Then suddenly he could not see them anymore. Suddenly they were hidden behind a swirling cloud of thick white smoke.

He could hear them still. He could hear their high, chittering shrieks of confusion and baffled hunger, hear the uneven flapping of their wings as they veered clumsily away from the smoke that drugged and slowed them.

For an instant, Rye thought he had lost his senses. This had happened at the Harbor! A cloud of smoke, just when it was needed! But where had smoke come from here — all the way up here, where there was nothing to make it, no one but . . . ?

And suddenly, Rye understood. Suddenly he understood many things. His eyes streaming, he turned his head and looked at Sonia. And through a veil of smoke he saw Sonia staring back at him defiantly, her eyes glittering green, sparks shooting from the hair that flew and crackled about her head like fire.

"Sonia!" he croaked. "The smoke . . . you . . ."

Sonia's grip on his hand tightened. He felt her voice.

Yes. But I cannot hold it in place much longer. We must go!

The images of towering trees, banks of ferns, and a rushing stream flashed into Rye's mind, so clearly and powerfully that they engulfed every other thought.

The feather, Rye! Now!

Then wind was howling in Rye's ears, and smoke was stinging his eyes. And the next moment, he was no longer high above Fell End, but deep in rustling darkness.

He knew Sonia was with him, and Farr, and Jett. He could feel them all. The skimmers had been left behind. The smoke had been left behind, too, though traces of its smell hung about him, mingling with the scents of damp earth and growing things.

The Fell Zone.

He became aware that he was still clutching the red feather, and stuffed it into his pocket. He would have liked to get rid of the armor shell and speed ring, too. It made him sick to feel them on his fingers. But he forced himself to leave them alone.

He felt Sonia's hand slide out of his. "We need light," she said stiffly. She pulled out the brown bag and thrust it at Rye. He unwound the broken cord from its neck and pulled out the crystal.

Light flooded the fern bank where they sat, and the stream that rushed beside them. It shone on Farr, still staring sightlessly ahead. It shone on Jett, crawling to his knees and looking around fearfully. It lit up Sonia's pale, expressionless face, her glowing emerald eyes, her hair glittering like tangled copper wires.

"Witch!" Jett hissed.

He lunged at Sonia, gibbering with hatred. Sonia's lip curled in contempt. And before he could lay a finger on her, Jett was writhing on the ground, groaning and fighting for breath.

Like the gray guard who attacked me at the Harbor, Rye thought.

Sonia nodded, very slightly.

Four-Eyes the trader's sudden headache after cheating the people of the Den . . . The slave hunter Kyte missing her aim again and again when she was trying to kill Sholto. The smoke. Your escape into the waiting room under the Warden's nose. The unlocking of the secret door. Jett's sudden sleep in the watchtower . . .

Again, that slight, stiff nod.

Rye took a deep breath, remembering. *The feather, so much more powerful when you are helping me . . .*

Tie Jett up, Rye. He is a danger to himself and to us. Use the cord.

"She is speaking to you in your mind," Jett cried hoarsely. "I can see it in your face! That is what Fellan do! By the Wall, Keelin, she has bewitched you! Fight her! She is our enemy! She is Fellan! Fellan!"

"I am not Fellan," said Sonia, pale as moonlight. "I am of Weld. I am an orphan of Weld."

"Who were your parents, then?" Jett demanded. "Name them! I challenge you to name them!"

"I do not have to answer to you, Jett of Northwall," Sonia answered coldly.

There was a roaring in Rye's ears. Numbly he began untangling the faded cord from Farr's ankles. He had to wrestle with it, but Farr seemed to feel nothing. He sat motionless and staring, like a dead man.

Bent over Farr, Rye could feel Sonia's eyes upon him. Confused thoughts were flitting through his mind one after the other. Sonia had powerful magic at her command. Sonia could see the Fell Zone paths. Sonia had led him to the meeting with Edelle and the other Fellan. Sonia had been able to find the Doors to Weld when no one else could see them. Sonia had made it her business to become close to the daughter of the Warden of Weld, and thus gained knowledge of the Weld volunteers.

It was with Sonia's help that Rye had caused the death of Olt.

Rye knew what Dirk would say if Dirk were here, on fire because his gullible young brother had been used as a pawn by the beings of the forbidden forest. He knew what Sholto would say, after putting his feelings aside and coolly considering the evidence.

But Rye looked straight into Sonia's green eyes, and smiled.

"And you do not have to answer to me," he said. "I know who you are. You are Sonia, and I would trust you with my life."

Sonia's tense face softened. Her pale lips parted in a long sigh. And Rye felt the icy shell that had held her rigid crack and melt away, and into his mind flooded the warmth of her overwhelming relief.

"The people of Weld were magic once, or so the old tales claim," he said softly. "Perhaps some of Dann's followers were part Fellan. Over time the magic faded, but it is still in our blood. No doubt it shows itself in a child every now and then, but inside the Wall it . . . is discouraged and kept hidden. Outside the Wall, it is set free."

Yes. Sonia sighed again. "I did not know it at first," she said aloud. "I had no idea why I felt so alive outside the Wall. I — I did things without realizing it, and then would be so tired I could not stay awake. It — was like using a muscle I had never used before, I suppose."

"But at the Harbor, in the testing hall, you understood what you could do."

The girl nodded, waiting.

"You saved us, but you did not tell us," Rye went on in a low voice. "You were afraid to tell — even me."

Pictures rushed from her mind into his. Some were memories: The Warden anxiously crossing his fingers and his wrists. A haggard woman shrieking in hatred. A small man shrinking away in fear. Jett's face, twisted with loathing. Some were imagined: Rye, Annocki, Sholto, Dirk, and Faene staring and pointing at the stranger among them.

Witch! Witch! Witch!

Rye straightened, holding the freed cord in his hands. "I understand," he said. "But it is a gift, Sonia, not a curse. Where would we have been without it?"

He drew breath, and made himself go on. "Sholto would agree," he added steadily. "Sholto does not trust magic, but — but he respects the truth. He would never blame anyone for being what they were born to be."

A sudden, frantic scuffle made them both jump. They swung around just in time to see Jett splash across the stream, plunge heedlessly into the undergrowth on the other side, and blunder away into the darkness.

"Let him go!" Sonia snapped as Rye made to follow. "If he prefers to risk the forest rather than stay with us, that is his choice! No matter what we say, he will never believe we mean him no harm. His mind is fixed. He is a true hero of Weld."

"What . . . is Weld?"

The voice was deep and puzzled. Rye and Sonia exchanged a startled glance, and turned to Farr.

Farr was sitting up, blinking and rubbing his forehead. "What — is Weld?" he asked again. "Where am I?" He caught sight of Rye and Sonia and his brow furrowed.

"You!" he hissed, trying to rise, feeling for the sword that no longer hung from his belt.

"Stay where you are, Chieftain Farr," Rye said hastily. "We are in the Fell Zone. Here you are safer with us than without us. It is night. The skimmers — the beasts you call slays — are abroad."

Farr stared at him, clearly trying to concentrate, to make sense of what had happened to him.

"Janna . . ." he managed to say.

"The lady Janna is safe in Fell End," Rye told him. "You do not need to fear for her."

Farr looked around. His eyes narrowed. "But it seems I should fear for myself."

"No!" Rye swallowed, hoping desperately that he could explain in a way the chieftain could understand. "We are not your enemies. We are not Fellan. We are your allies!"

"You've regained your memory, then, Keelin," Farr said drily. "You know who you are, at last."

"I have regained most of my memory, but not all," Rye said. "I still do not remember the moments just before the beast attacked Zak."

"How convenient." Farr's face was expressionless, but his every nerve was alert; Rye could feel it.

"My name is Rye," Rye went on doggedly. "Sonia and I came here to try to stop the skimmers — the slays. They prey on our home, too. We had no idea that they rose from the Fell Zone until we saw them take flight tonight."

"Why have you brought me here?" Farr asked tonelessly.

"To save you from the skimmers," Sonia said. "They do not hunt on the floor of the forest. The Fellan prevent it."

Farr cocked an eyebrow. "And how do you know that, if you are not Fellan yourself?"

"I just know it," Sonia muttered.

"Indeed." Farr straightened his shoulders and seemed to make a decision. Rye could feel his tension, his muffled fear and his determination. There was a strange sort of excitement, too. It was as if the man had vowed to follow a perilous path without knowing where that path might lead.

And perhaps, Rye thought slowly, *I should do the same. The risk is great, but it is worth taking.*

Beware, Rye, Sonia whispered in his mind. *Do not trust him!*

"Very well," Farr said loudly. "You've captured me, Keelin. You've brought me here. Now what's to be done?"

Rye took a breath. "I have something to show you," he said, untying the red bundle at his belt. "Something that Carryl would have liked you to see."

He pulled the gold casket from its wrapping, opened it, and displayed the glimmering disc to Farr.

Farr stared at the disc but made no attempt to touch it. "So," he murmured, "it does exist. Carryl told me, but I didn't believe her."

Suddenly he looked inexpressibly sad.

"You have been planning to attack the Fellan," Rye said. "Carryl did not want you to do it."

Farr sighed. "She believed it would be wrong. Dangerous. She said there was an ancient treaty — a spell that bound both parties. Well —" He shrugged his powerful shoulders. "We all heard that tale in our youth. Dorne's a strange island, with a strange history. Legends are bound to grow up in such a place."

"But this is not a legend." Bracing himself, Rye picked up the disc. It burned in his hand. Its surface rippled and the words appeared.

When I was born,
The spell was cast.
While I endure,
The Pledge will last.

Farr stared silently at the rhyme. Gradually his eyes hardened and he turned away.

"Fine words! But the spell has worn out, it seems. The Fellan broke their pledge when they began sending those creatures of sorcery to prey on us."

"The skimmers are no more creatures of sorcery than fell-dragons or bloodhogs are," Sonia said quietly. "And the Fellan did not breed them. They could well claim that they have not broken their pledge in deed, even if they have broken it in spirit."

"Again, you'd know that better than I would," Farr muttered, without turning around.

"And do not forget that the charm has been lost for centuries," Rye urged. "It was hidden away in a wall, behind a statue made of iron. It is possible that the Fellan could no longer sense it fully. Metal affects their magic."

"That I do know." There was a grim note in Farr's voice. The back of his neck was stiff, his shoulders tense.

Rye thought of the metal barrier fence, the metal slay shields. Yes, Farr and his people had done what they could to protect themselves from the Fellan. They relied upon metal as those in Weld who followed the old ways relied on salt to protect them from evil magic. But salt and metal would not ward off the Master. The Lord of Shadows had grown too powerful, too ancient in wickedness, for that.

The disc was scorching his fingers. Hastily he returned it to the casket. The rippling words vanished, but he knew they were there, hidden as the Fellan were hidden in the depths of their forest.

"It is not too late to mend this," he said urgently. "The spell endures while the charm endures — and the charm is here! It can save us all, Chieftain Farr . . . if only you will listen to me!"

THE POOL

Farr did not turn, but neither did he make an angry reply. He remained silent, waiting. Rye felt his mouth grow dry. What he had to say was so important, and time was so short, that he hardly knew how to begin. If only he could speak as persuasively as Dirk — or as Farr himself!

Well, there is no point in crying after things I cannot have, he thought. *All I can do is to keep the story as simple as possible and trust Farr to recognize the truth when he hears it.*

"Attacking the Fellan will not help your people — or our people either, Chieftain Farr," he began. "The Fellan are not acting alone. Olt is dead. His death has allowed his brother, the evil sorcerer they call the Lord of Shadows, to invade the east of Dorne and take control of the exiles' settlement there. The Lord of Shadows is using jell to breed skimmers — slays — that can attack by day as well as by night."

The muscles in the back of Farr's neck twitched as if he was about to speak, but he seemed to think better of it, and remained silent.

Wishing he could see the man's face, Rye made himself go on.

"You will never defeat the Lord of Shadows by force of arms. You need powerful magic on your side. You need the Fellan! They are our only chance, but if you attack them tomorrow, you yourself will have broken the treaty, and the chance will be lost forever."

As he spoke, the thought of the pipeline flitted across his mind. He knew now that the pipe and the tubing attached to it were not to be used to deliver skimmers to Weld. What, then, was their purpose? He longed to ask, but did not dare. The question might well convince Farr that he was a Fellan spy after all.

"I see," Farr said tonelessly. "You advise me to cancel the attack, Keelin, defying my council and acting against the will of my people. And then what?"

"Then you come back into the Fell Zone with me, we meet the Fellan face-to-face, and we confront them with this!" Rye pointed to the disc. "When it is before their eyes, they will be forced to accept that they are still bound by their pledge. They will have no choice but to join with us and help us to defeat the enemy."

For a long moment, Farr did not move, and as the silence lengthened, Rye became aware that the forest, too, had become very still. There was not a sound except the rushing of the stream. His skin prickled.

Why have you returned, Rye of Weld? You are not wanted here!

Leave him be! He is the one! He will do what he must.

The Fellan voices hissed in Rye's mind. They were coming from somewhere upstream, he was sure of it. He glanced at Sonia, but she had felt nothing, it seemed. She was watching Farr's rigid back, her eyes very grave.

Then, abruptly, Farr turned to face them.

"Very well," he said. "I'll do as you ask, with one small change in the order of things. We've the whole night ahead of us. Take me to the Fellan now! We'll show them the charm and see what they make of it. If they convince me they'll move to my side, I'll cancel the attack. Not before."

We have nothing to say to the human who wishes to make war on us, just as we had nothing to say to the six who came before him only to die in the nets of fell-dragons. Remove him from our place, Rye of Weld!

Leave him be! Trust! He carries the Sign.

We have trusted too long!

This time the whispers pierced Rye's mind like arrows. Tears of pain sprang into his eyes. He bowed his head, fighting not to let Farr see what he was feeling.

You will speak to the chieftain! he told the Fellan furiously. *By this token, you must!* He wiped his eyes, snatched the disc from the casket, and held it high. The charm flashed in the light of the crystal and the words on the rippling surface seemed to writhe. The whispering voices fell silent.

"Well?" Farr demanded.

"I will lead you to them," Rye replied. "Take hold of my shoulder, and you will be safe from harm."

Rye, beware! Sonia's message was sharp with fear and warning.

There is nothing else to be done, Rye answered briefly.

He cast the gold casket aside and slid the disc into his pocket. Then he drew the bell tree stick from his belt, and with it and the light crystal held in front of him, led the way upstream.

They walked in silence, the stream rushing away beside them. Once before, Rye and Sonia had followed a Fell Zone stream, but this time the experience was very different. This time the water was no babbling companion, traveling in the same direction they were. This time they were walking upstream instead of down, and though they were on dry land, their steps dragged as if they were wading against a strong, invisible tide.

And this time there were no stealthy rustlings in the undergrowth that lined the stream banks, and no unseen creatures howled and screeched. The stillness was unearthly. It was as if the whole of the forbidden forest was waiting — and waiting in dread.

It was like walking in a dream. The light of the crystal was like a bubble that enclosed them. The rushing of the stream filled Rye's mind, drowning thought, drowning even fear.

And suddenly the sense of being in a dream was overwhelming. For without warning, the stream vanished under a shelf of rock, and Rye found himself entering a mossy clearing with a small, dark pool in its center.

How can this be?

Rye felt Sonia's shock echo his own. He stood stock-still, gazing around in confusion and fear. How could it be that they had arrived at the same place where they had first met the Fellan, beyond the golden Door?

Then, very slowly, Rye saw that there were differences between this clearing and the one where he had received the bag of powers. This clearing was a little smaller. The towering ferns that surrounded it were taller, their shaggy brown trunks were thicker, and their lacy fronds masked more of the starry sky. The moss underfoot was richer and greener — more like a velvet cushion than a carpet.

And the feeling . . . the feeling was very different. The Fellan beyond the golden Door had been wary, certainly, but they had wanted him to find them. The hidden beings who were watching him now resented his presence and wished him gone.

"What is it?" Farr muttered behind him, pressing

forward. "Why have you —?" He broke off so abruptly that Rye glanced quickly back at him. The chieftain's strong face was beaded with sweat. He was bent forward, as if bracing himself against a gale.

"They will not let him in," Sonia said.

Rye gritted his teeth in frustration. "Wait here at the edge, Chieftain Farr," he said in a low voice. "We will try to make them see reason."

Farr nodded sullenly and stumbled a few steps back till he was no longer standing on the moss.

Reflecting grimly that the peace meeting had not begun well, Rye made himself walk with Sonia to the edge of the pool. The light of the crystal flooded the gleaming surface of the water.

And suddenly he knew, with a surge of exaltation, that he was exactly where he should be — where he should have been long ago. Here, in this clearing beyond the wooden Door, were the answers he had been seeking. The watching Fellan might not want him here, but something more ancient did.

He knelt by the pool, drew the disc from his pocket, and held it high. As the disc's surface rippled, the water rippled, too.

"What must I do?" he asked quietly.

Instantly, the ripples in the pool formed themselves into words.

Guard the heart

"What does it mean?" Sonia whispered. "Whose heart must we guard?"

Rye swallowed. "I think . . . *this* is the heart," he said. "The heart of Dorne. The Fell Zone."

He looked over his shoulder. Farr was a dark shadow at the edge of the clearing. The chieftain was watching, no doubt, but he would not be able to see the words in the pool from where he stood.

And even if Farr could see them, they would not change his mind. To Farr, they would be nothing but an attempt by the Fellan to avoid attack without making any promises.

And perhaps that was all they were. Perhaps the feeling of rightness Rye had felt as he looked down into the pool was just another Fellan trick.

Rye turned back to the pool, disappointment sour in his stomach. The words had faded away. The water was mirror smooth again, and all he could see in it was the dim, mysterious reflection of his own face.

The floating image seemed to mock him. He could not bear it. On impulse he swept the bell tree stick through it, and with fierce satisfaction saw it vanish as the surface of the pool shivered into a thousand broken ripples.

The Sign. At last . . .

The words of the Fellan hissed in his mind like a gust of cool, tingling breath.

Then his heart gave a great thud. Pictures were

forming in the broken water — the ghostly, moving images of three young men with flaming red hair.

The first man was tall, handsome, and broad-shouldered. The second was slighter, with secretive eyes and a proud tilt to his head. The third, clearly the youngest, looked eager and loving.

Rye knew who they were. He knew it without a doubt. They were the three sorcerer brothers whose tale was told in the ancient book he carried beneath his shirt. Why had their images come here, to him?

The pictures in the water grew sharper. And now Rye could see every fold of the men's rich cloaks, and every line on the three faces that were so alike and yet so different. He could see that the two older brothers were arguing violently, while the youngest stood silently by. And then, as he watched, the youngest slowly turned, raised a hand beseechingly, and looked directly at him.

In panic, Rye snatched the stick from the water. Instantly the pictures vanished.

Rye, what is happening?

Rye glanced at Sonia, met her frightened eyes. He realized that she had glimpsed the images in his mind but had seen nothing in the pool — nothing but ripples.

"Pictures — in the water," he managed to say. "The three brothers."

As he spoke, he shivered, remembering the gaze of the youngest brother. And yet . . . why was he afraid?

There had been nothing unfriendly in those steady eyes, nothing threatening in that raised hand. There had only been appeal — mute, urgent appeal.

Plainly something was wanted of him. There was something he had to see — something he had to know.

He looked at the stick hanging, dripping, in his hand. Between the finger and thumb of the same hand, he held the disc, the charm he had hoped would save them all.

But the charm had not called the images into the water. The stick had done that — the bell tree stick, so smooth, fitting his hand so well. He had carried it from home, carried it all this way. It had not been much of a weapon. But he had kept it with him anyway, and now he knew why.

We were given three signs by which we would know the one we awaited, the Fellan Edelle had said when she had given him the bag of powers.

Three signs. The third and last had been that Rye could drink from the pool called Dann's Mirror. But what of the other two? Rye had been so sure Edelle was mistaken, and the magic she was giving him was intended for someone else, that he had not bothered to think about what they might have been.

Now he did. And now, remembering some of the other things the Fellan beyond the golden Door had said, he felt he knew.

The first sign had been that he had brought magic with him — Sonia, in whose veins the blood of the

Fellan ran so strongly. And the second had been that he carried a stick from a bell tree — the rare little tree that the Sorcerer Dann had loved and used as his emblem.

The stick was a symbol, and by it the Fellan had known him. The serpents of Oltan had known him by it, too, when he had held it high on the rock of sacrifice, the magic scale glimmering in the palm of his other hand. The beast at Fell End had recoiled from it. The gold and silver Doors had known it, and at its touch had opened to let him back into Weld.

"Here," Rye said, thrusting the disc at Sonia. She took it in surprise but very gladly, her eyes lighting up as if reflecting the charm's magic gleam. In her hand, it shone more brilliantly than ever, its surface changing rapidly from blue to green, green to blue, and if it was burning her fingers she made no sign of it.

And Rye took a firmer grip on the bell tree stick and plunged it again into the pool.

THE THREE BROTHERS

The water began to swirl in broad circles as if Rye had stirred it. It swirled as if it was rushing down a drain, around and around till it made a funnel that reached down into the pool's depths. Around the edges of the funnel, the water was churned into foam. But deep in the center, there was a still, round space where terrible pictures flickered.

The two older sorcerer brothers were dueling in a great room where the dead body of an old man lay in state. Their shadows leaped wildly on the walls as killing spells flashed fire, and the flames of the tall candles around the bier bent and flared.

Rye's heart was beating so fast that he could hardly breathe. He pressed the hand that held the light crystal to his chest. The ruined book beneath his shirt seemed to warm. And suddenly words floated into his mind — words he had never read, but which now came to him as if he could see them before his eyes.

❖   When Chieftain Perry died, it was understood that Annoltis, his eldest son, would take his place as leader, for Annoltis was dearly loved by the people. But Malverlain, the second son, was bitterly jealous. He believed that his great knowledge of dark sorcery gave him the right to rule, and cursed the fools who preferred his brother to him. In his rage, he attacked Annoltis, intending murder.

Annoltis. Malverlain. Those names . . . Rye's scalp crawled. Beside him, Sonia had become unnaturally still. He could not have shielded his mind even if he had wanted to, and he knew she was sharing his visions, seeing the names through him.

He saw the eldest brother beaten back. He saw the savage triumph on the face of the Sorcerer Malverlain change to shock as a shadow moved to the staggering Annoltis's side. Again words shone in his mind.

❖   But Malverlain had forgotten that he did not have one brother only, but two. He had forgotten Eldannen, the youngest, whose quiet ways masked a power that was very great. Eldannen's bond with the Fellan was as strong as Malverlain's own secret dread of them, and the Fellan had taught him well. When Eldannen joined Annoltis in battle, Malverlain was lost.

Eldannen. His mind whirling in confusion, Rye saw Malverlain fleeing into exile in a boat with a gray sail marked in red. He saw the eldest brother and the youngest standing on the shore, holding the banishing spell between them. He saw the people creeping out of hiding, rejoicing because they had been saved and their beloved Annoltis was triumphant.

Faster the water spun, and faster. Deep within the frame of foam, pictures of the past flashed by, years passing in the blink of an eye. Annoltis ruled as chieftain, Eldannen by his side. The brothers grew older and older, living, like their mother's people, far beyond the normal span of human years.

Then Annoltis began to weaken, and as he weakened, he changed. His orders became shriller and more impatient. He began spending his time alone, studying ancient books. His fiery hair had grown scant and white, and his broad shoulders were bowed with age. But as he mumbled over the old texts, his eyes still burned with a will to live that was even fiercer than before.

And at last, there came a time when he scurried down dark stone steps, clutching something that glimmered under his cloak. Torches burst into flaming life as he crept along a passageway carved with the images of beasts, to a cavity where an iron statue of a sea serpent swallowing its own tail seemed to squirm like a live thing.

Annoltis raised his mottled hand. With a grating sound, the statue slid out of the cavity, revealing a blank wall thick with spiderweb. Another gesture, and the outline of a small door appeared in the grimy stones. The door swung open. With a cackle, Annoltis drew a gold casket from beneath his cloak.

Watching feverishly, Rye caught his breath.

"Why are you hiding the charm down here, brother? Surely it was safer where it was, with you?"

Rye could hear the words as clearly as he could see the figure that had appeared beside Annoltis in the passageway. They were not words from the book, he was sure of it. The author of the book had not known where the casket had been hidden.

Suddenly, it seemed, Rye was hearing the past as well as seeing it. And that had to mean that what was to come was of vital importance. He leaned forward, straining his ears, narrowing his stinging eyes.

Annoltis spun around, scowling, to face Eldannen. Eldannen's beard was gray, but the years had dealt more kindly with him than they had with his brother, for there was nothing grasping or secret in his face.

"I no longer care to have the charm by me," snapped Annoltis. "It disturbs my work."

"That is because your 'work' is taking you into evil places," Eldannen replied gravely. "The charm disturbs you because dark magic is corrupting you, as long ago it corrupted our brother Malverlain."

An expression like horror flickered across the chieftain's face. Then conceit settled back over his features like a mask, and the moment had passed.

"You have never understood the needs and burdens of leadership, Eldannen," he rasped. "You have always wanted the world to be better and kinder than it can ever be." A nerve twitched in his withered cheek. "It comes from being the youngest and our mother's darling, no doubt. Her Fellan dreams infected you in the cradle."

Scowling, he thrust the casket into the hole in the wall. He watched the door seal itself, then stepped out into the passageway. At once, the metal statue slid back into place, filling the cavity once more.

"You are taking a fearful risk, Annoltis," Eldannen said in a low voice. "The charm must never be lost or forgotten. Our father's treaty . . ."

"The treaty will be kept wherever the charm may lie," Annoltis snapped. "I am chieftain. I will see to it."

"But what of the chieftains who come after you?"

Annoltis grinned. His shadowed face looked like a skull. "There will be no chieftains after me, brother," he whispered. "At last, I have found a way. The blood of the young will preserve my life. The first Gifting will be on Midsummer Eve."

Rye's heart seemed to stop. He felt Sonia seize his hand.

"The blood of the young," Eldannen repeated dully. "Oh, Olt, how could you, the best of men, have come to this?"

"Shut your mouth!" the tyrant shouted. "And do not call me what the people call me! We are brothers! You know my true name — use it!"

Eldannen's eyes were bleak. "Annoltis," he said, "I cannot stand by while you do this evil thing."

"What?" Olt stormed. "Am I to die while across the sea Malverlain lives on and grows in power every day? Am I to die and rot when I have found a way to prevent it?"

"Your way is monstrous," said Eldannen.

For a long moment, Olt stood struggling to calm himself, then he drew himself up. "It is necessary," he said stiffly. "My life is more important than other lives. Will you fight me over it?"

Eldannen shook his head. "You know I will never raise my hand against you, brother. But I must go."

It seemed to Rye that Olt paled. But again, the moment of weakness passed quickly and his face twisted into a sneer.

"Indeed!" he spat. "And what of the part-Fellan scum you insist on calling friends? Will you leave them to my tender mercies?"

"No," Eldannen said quietly. "I will take them with me — all who wish to come. I have thought of this for a long time, Annoltis, even planned for it, but I have stayed by your side, telling myself that my influence must at last prevail with you. I see now that I was wrong. My followers and I will begin a new life, in a new place. And for the sake of the love that was once between us, brother, you will not prevent it."

Annoltis rubbed his mouth with the back of his hand, perhaps to hide the trembling of his lips. "I will not prevent it," he said sullenly. "But know this, Eldannen! If you leave me, I will curse you as a traitor. I will make it a crime to utter your name. I will erase all mention of you from every book and document within my reach. It will be as if you had never been born!"

"So be it," said Eldannen, and to Rye's amazement, there was pity as well as sadness in his voice. "But I give you a solemn warning in return. Your flatterers may tell you that Dorne needs you at any price, but the people will not agree. The people will rise against you, and destroy you."

"No, they will not!" Annoltis shrieked. "They will not dare. Because I am going to make them believe that only my life stands between them and the revenge of Malverlain!"

Rye's mind was like a raging whirlpool. He knew that Sonia was sharing his tumult, but he could not turn to her. He could not drag his eyes from the pictures in the water.

Eldannen was staring at his brother as if he could hardly believe what he had heard. "You . . . you would tell this lie, knowing how dangerous it could be?"

"There is no danger!" Olt cried. "Why should anyone find out the truth?" His eyes narrowed. "Unless you tell them — you, who learned our father's secret by stealth!"

Abruptly he looked murderous.

"Your secret is no secret among the Fellan," Eldannen said quietly. "To them, it is a simple fact of life. If they had not lived hidden away for so long, everyone in Dorne would know it as well as I do."

"Perhaps," growled Olt. "As it is, I am safe."

"But Dorne is not," his brother murmured. "That is the danger I meant, Annoltis. What if you die at last, despite your vile plan? If you have not passed our father's secret on, there will be no one left alive who knows that it is vital to guard the heart of Dorne. There will be no one who knows that the charmed circle protecting this island was never your doing, but is held in place by the Fellan!"

Guard the heart. The Fellan . . .

Rye swayed forward as a dizzying wave of heat swept through him. Sonia's hand tightened on his, steadying him, pulling him back.

"Leave here, Enemy!" Olt howled at his brother. "Leave here now or you and your scurvy friends will not live to see another sunrise!"

The water at the pool's edge swirled and foamed. The pictures in the center began to move faster, faster. And now Rye was seeing things that made no sense, things that defied reason.

Eldannen was fleeing the dark city, a bright light held high before him and a long string of people gliding behind him, hand in hand. . . .

Eldannen was moving through low hills, and the line behind him was a little longer. The sky above was faintly tinged with the pink of sunrise. He lifted his hand, pulled a hood over his head, and he and his followers vanished. . . .

Eldannen and his people, visible once more, were threading their way through enormous trees, climbing toward a cave that yawned in the rock of a mountaintop. Shadowy green figures flitted around them, and the beasts of the forest stayed away. . . .

Eldannen was entering the cave and passing through it to a heavy wooden door bound with brass. He was tapping a smooth stick on the door, and the door was swinging open. He was standing back as his followers passed through the doorway two by two. And at last, he was raising his hand in farewell to the Fellan and passing through himself, the door swinging shut behind him.

Rye gaped, his mind reeling.

Olt's youngest brother, friend of the Fellan, had led his followers not to the east, but to Weld. Olt's brother Eldannen, who had fled into exile just before the first Gifting, had been the Sorcerer Dann.

But Rye and Sonia had arrived in Oltan just before the second Gifting, only seven years later. And by then Weld had existed for centuries.

Or so its people believed.

Rye shuddered all over. He wanted to pull the bell tree stick out of the water, turn his face away from the pool, but he could not move. He felt Sonia lose her way, lose her connection with him. And then the pictures were flashing through his burning eyes to his numbed brain so fast that he could do nothing but stare, clinging helplessly to Sonia's cold hand while above the clearing the sky lightened and the stars began to fade.

When he came to himself, he was lying on the moss with no memory of falling away from the pool. He thought back to the pictures he had seen in the water, and his mind recoiled. No. He could not think about them yet. Not yet.

Sonia was slumped beside him and the bell tree stick was drying in his hand. The light crystal was still clutched in his other hand, but the armor shell had slipped from his finger. Numbly he pushed it back into place.

He turned his head and saw Farr sitting with his back to a tree fern, head bowed. So Farr had kept faith. He had waited through the long night till at last he had fallen asleep.

There was a faint sound high above. Rye looked up, and his stomach lurched. The patch of sky glimmering between the feathery tips of the giant ferns was dark with skimmers. The skimmers were returning from their hunt, hastening to their nest in the Fell Zone, fleeing the rising sun.

The skimmers. Here, at least, was something Rye could understand. Here was something real to cling to, the reason he, Sonia, Dirk, and Sholto had left Weld in the first place.

The main part of the skimmer swarm had already passed overhead. Only a few ragged shapes now flapped across the lightening sky. There was no time to lose.

Rye scrambled up. He thrust the stick in his belt, pushed the light crystal into his pocket, and took out the feather. *Up!* he thought. And then he was rising slowly past the shaggy brown trunks of the vast ferns, rising through the lacy fronds that nodded against the green-gray sky, rising high above the crowns of the mighty trees beyond. . . .

And he was watching the skimmers going to roost. He was staring at something he had to fight to believe. His heart was hammering in his chest. His throat was closing. . . .

And then the beasts were gone, hidden, safe for another day. The blinding rays of the rising sun were streaking across the sky. And with the sun came a sudden, shocking burst of sound from the forest edge — barked orders, the clatter of falling metal, the thud of booted feet, and a low, dangerous roar that raised the hairs on the back of Rye's neck.

He faltered in the air, lost height, managed to steady himself only by a huge effort of will. His eyes dazzled and streaming, he looked down, toward Fell

End. Beneath the high arch of the pipeline, two long sections of the metal fence had been flattened. Helmeted figures, clad from head to foot in gleaming white, were tramping over the metal sheets, their clumsy weapons roaring as they blasted the undergrowth ahead with flame. Brown smoke billowed upward, tainting the clear morning air.

We are betrayed. . . .

The Fellan voices came to Rye like the wail of the wind. His heart in his mouth, he plummeted down, down into the clearing where the giant ferns were thrashing as if beaten by a gale.

Sonia was standing by the pool, staring at Farr, who had risen to his feet. In her hand was the disc, the token of the treaty, glowing so brightly that her skin seemed drenched with green.

"Farr!" Rye bellowed. "Stop them! Stop —"

A distant chorus of shouts rose from below. The whole forest seemed to shudder. And Sonia screamed as the disc of the treaty shattered, and its fragments, fine as glittering dust, wafted away in air that shimmered with Fellan pain and rage.

TERROR

The chieftain stood up. His eyes were hard, his mouth set in a tight half smile, and suddenly, with sick dismay, Rye saw the truth. Farr had known all along that the attack would go on without him. Farr had planned for everything, including his own capture or death. "Nothing must stop us now," he must have said to Manx, Barron, and Sigrid as they left Riverside. "You are to move at sunrise whether I am with you to give the order or not."

Farr had never trusted Rye — had not believed a word Rye said. He had agreed to go deeper into the forest, to go almost certainly to his own death, only to make the Fellan feel safe and give his soldiers the advantage of surprise.

There was another roar from below, and another. The sky above the clearing was dark with smoke. Sonia covered her face and swayed where she stood.

Rye ran to her and caught her before she fell. She sagged against him, her mind clouded, her whole body trembling.

"You fool!" he shrieked at Farr. "Do you know what you have done?"

"I've done what I had to do," Farr snapped back. "And if I'm a fool, Keelin, you're a greater one. How could you expect me to believe that the Shadow Lord had invaded Dorne without my knowing it? Why, when I first saw you at Fell End, I had just returned from touring the east coast guard posts and seen for myself that all was well!"

Rye gaped at him over Sonia's head, his mind frozen, his teeth chattering.

Farr raised his eyebrows, and his face softened slightly. "Can it be that you really believe the nonsense you told me?" he murmured. "Yes, I see you do. So you're a dupe, Keelin, not a villain! It's said that the Fellan can create illusions, make people see —"

He broke off with a start. Hooded figures were peeling away from the swaying trunks of the giant ferns. Their garments flew in the wind of their fury, their hoods blew back, and their long braids twisted and hissed around their heads like spitting snakes. Their bodies seemed to flicker as their color changed from brown to green.

"You have broken the treaty of our ancestors, human," a female rasped at Farr. "You have invaded our land. Your people will pay the price."

Farr raised his chin. "My troops know their danger, Fellan," he said evenly. "As one man falls, another will take his place. You won't stop us. You won't defeat us. You and your cursed magic are finished!"

The Fellan looked at him, their eyes burning. He groaned and fell to his knees.

"Do not harm him!" Rye burst out. "He is the only one who can stop the attack! Make him understand! Tell him that it is only because you allowed it that the Lord of Shadows was able to invade! Tell him —"

He quailed as the Fellan turned on him, contempt in their green eyes. Their voices hissed in his mind.

You insult us, Rye of Weld! Lies and empty threats are for humans, not for the Fellan. The Sorcerer Malverlain will never return to claim Dorne. Never, while we live!

"But — but he *has* invaded!" Rye stammered. "Beyond the silver Door. I saw — we saw —"

The green eyes flashed. To his amazement, Rye saw in them what looked like shock and fear. The air of the clearing seemed to blur. Then the Fellan were gone.

Rye could not think. His mind felt numb. Sonia was struggling to stand upright, and Farr was striding toward him, but he could not move. Screams of terror had begun rising from below. Farr's face seemed to swirl before him in a mist. The chieftain's lips were moving, but it seemed to take a long time before the words came to Rye's ears.

"Take me out of here, I tell you!" Farr barked, seizing his arm and shaking it. "I must see — I must know. . . ."

Rye looked down at his hand. He was still clutching the red feather. He remembered floating above the treetops as the sun rose, only minutes ago. He remembered what he had seen. Instantly his mind recoiled, taking refuge in numbness once more.

Rye! Do as he says!

Sonia's silent cry filtered through the muffling wall that seemed to have enclosed Rye's mind. He forced himself to respond.

"Only if you agree to have your hands tied," he said to Farr, his voice sounding to his own ears like the voice of a stranger. "You are not to be trusted."

Without a word, Farr held out his hands, wrists together.

Rye glanced at Sonia. She hesitated for an instant, then pulled the piece of cord from her waist and looped it around the man's wrists. He stiffened and his eyes went blank.

"Stop pretending, Farr!" Rye snapped. "That trick will not work a second time."

"He is not pretending," Sonia said quietly. "Do you not see, Rye? It is the cord."

As Rye swung around to her, she shrugged. "I found it long ago, hidden away in an old cupboard in the Keep tower," she murmured. "I — liked it, though I did not know why, and I have kept it by me ever since.

I — I think now that it is made of Fellan hair. It does not affect me, but for people with no Fellan blood, like Farr, it must be different. It — it stills them."

Rye shook his head in disbelief. If only they had known the cord's power before!

"Like the powers in the bag," Sonia said, touching her pocket where the damaged bag lay hidden. "We had to work them out one by one. And we still do not know what the ninth power is, or what the honey sweet can —"

She froze as the terrible sounds from below suddenly grew louder. Quickly, Rye slipped his arm through Farr's, pulled the hood over his head, and raised the feather. He felt Sonia's magic rush into his fingertips. And the next instant, he was opening his eyes on a nightmare.

At first, he almost believed he was back in the Diggings. The ground was flooded in weird yellow light. Gray cloud blanketed the sky. Whips cracked, and flames leaped. Groans and screams filled the air. Great carts pulled by teams of grunting hogs labored over seared earth. Everywhere there were helmeted figures dressed in gray.

But as the smoke swirled, clearing in patches only to close in again, Rye came to his senses. Of course this was not the Diggings. It was the Fell Zone, burning.

He, Sonia, and Farr were standing behind a scorched tree, halfway up the burned black track that the troops with flamers had already created in their march uphill. It was smoke that was muffling the sky. The figures were not gray guards but Farr's troops, their protective suits heavily filmed with ash. The carts were not laden with broken rocks, but piled high with barrels. And the screams were not the cries of tormented slaves but the terrible sounds of soldiers dying hideously beneath the teeth and claws of enraged fell-dragons that sprang hissing from the trees.

Rye turned his face away. He could not look. "Untie the cord, Sonia!" he shouted, his voice breaking. "Free Farr, so he can call his troops back!"

"He will not call them back," Sonia said, barely moving her lips. "He knows they can win."

And when Rye made himself look again at the terrible scene, he saw that it was so. Farr's troops were dying, but fell-dragons were dying, too, as soldiers sprang to defend their fallen comrades. Savage as the giant lizards were, they could not stand forever against swords, arrows, spears, and flame.

Tails lashing in fury, the beasts lunged at their attackers, killing and maiming wherever they could. But the soldiers were too many. Their weapons were too strong. Their rage made them fearless.

His throat aching, his eyes stinging, Rye saw lizard after lizard crash to the scorched ground, its jaws still dripping with the blood of its last victim. With every creature's death, a great wave of Fellan pain burst into his mind, crashing against the bitter tide of triumph streaming from the soldiers who had avenged their friends.

And as Farr had predicted, the attack did not falter, for every soldier who fell was instantly replaced by another. Shoulder to shoulder, their helmeted heads bent against the wind, the troops with flame weapons were moving doggedly upward, setting fire to everything in their path. Behind them, on the broad black strip that now climbed from the broken barrier like a ragged, smoking road, the dead and injured were being lifted onto stretchers and carried away. The carts trundled on, veering left and right to avoid the scorched trees and the bodies of the slaughtered dragons, the hogs squealing and showing the whites of their eyes at the scent of blood.

Yet no figure with flashing green eyes and hair like flame flew to stop the army's advance with a flick of a hand. No soldier fell by magic or froze as if bewitched. The ground fire burned unchecked, rising higher and higher up the hill. The carts rolled on without hindrance. And slowly Rye understood that this was because the Fellan were nowhere near. The Fellan had retreated, as if repelled by some force they could not fight.

The carts.

Rye turned to Sonia as her message came to him. She nodded slightly, her eyes dull.

A great gust of wind howled around them, almost lifting them off their feet. The Fellan could not approach the track, perhaps, but they had the wind at their command, and the wind was fearful. It was screaming like a live thing, raging through the treetops, filling the air with choking smoke and ash, sending flaming twigs and embers flying back toward Fell End. The Fellan were turning Farr's own weapon against him.

And suddenly, despite what she had said, Sonia was fumbling with the cord looped around Farr's wrists and pulling it away.

"Stop the attack!" she cried to Farr, who blinked at her, dazed, as if he had just woken from a deep sleep. "Do you not see what is happening? Fell End will burn! Everyone will die! Your wife! Your people! Rye's —" Her voice broke off in a choking sob.

Rye's brothers . . .

Dirk. Sholto. Stiffly, Rye turned his head, looked down at the town. People with scarves tied over their mouths and noses packed the riverbank. They were passing water-filled buckets from hand to hand, quenching flying sparks and embers as they fell, drenching the ground, the dock, the houses, in preparation for what might come.

"Fell End will survive," Farr muttered, though Rye could feel his fear. "The first stage is almost complete. Any moment now . . ."

And as he spoke, a vast crashing and clattering began. The leading carts had stopped and begun shedding their loads. Soldiers were pushing the barrels over the sides. The barrels were thudding onto the blackened ground, bursting open so that their contents spilled and scattered.

Rye's throat closed as he saw the objects rolling and coming to rest on the scorched ground. Bent metal rods. Scraps of roofing iron. Twisted metal shutters. Broken tools and weapons. Rusted anchors. Odd lengths of chain and wire. Even small household items like burned-out kettles, dented buckets, and cooking pots that had lost their handles.

Waste metal, collected from every warehouse, every shop, farm, and home in New Nerra and beyond. Metal to quench the magic of the Fellan.

This was why the guardians of the forest had retreated. This was why the soldiers had only the fell-dragons and the wind to fight as they burned their way up to the Fell Zone's summit.

And the more metal was brought in, the less the Fellan would be able to defend this part of their territory. Even now, the mighty wind was wavering, weakening, and cheers were rising from Fell End, from the soldiers leading the hogs that drew the carts, from the troops with the flamers.

Farr gave a great sigh. Rye turned to him. The chieftain's face was slack with relief.

"You could not quite believe it would work," Rye said evenly.

Farr wiped the sweat from his brow. "It seemed

such a simple thing," he admitted. "But I was well advised. Now we've a safe place to begin."

I was well advised.

The words floated into Rye's mind and clung there like prickling burrs as troops pounced on the objects littering the track and hurled them far into the undergrowth. They clung there as the first carts emptied and other carts trundled past them to shed their loads farther up the hill. They clung there as Rye felt the Fellan's power shrink back, and as the wind beating on his face gradually stuttered and died.

And only then, in what seemed a sudden, deathly hush, did Rye focus on Farr's last words.

Now we've a safe place to begin.

THREE DOORS

Fire and metal were only part of Farr's plan. There was something worse to come. Rye could see that in the chieftain's tired but exultant face, in the determined tilt of his chin. And in that moment Rye realized it was the charm, the token of the treaty, that had made Farr hesitate to attack the Fellan for so long. Farr had not known the disc existed, but it had still exerted power over him. Now it was gone, and all the man's doubts had gone with it.

"Farr," Rye cried desperately. "I beg you, stop the attack. The Fellan keep Dorne safe — safe from invasion! I saw it in the pool. They —"

Farr shook his head pityingly. "Get away from here, Keelin," he muttered. "Find somewhere safe to hide till your mind's your own again."

He pulled himself free and strode out of cover. Smoke and ash swirled around him. The men trudging by with the carts did not notice him, and he made no effort to attract their attention. He merely stood and waited, looking down toward Fell End.

Stop him, Rye!

Sonia's thought was as faint as a sigh. She was leaning heavily on Rye's arm, perhaps hardly knowing what she did. The great weight of metal hidden in the passing carts was sapping more of her energy every moment. Her eyes were as dull as they had been in the wasteland of the Saltings.

Rye drew her closer, trying to strengthen her with his warmth. And with a mixture of admiration and pity, he felt her rousing herself, fighting to respond.

The Enemy . . . he felt her call to him. *The Enemy . . . the pipeline . . .*

Rye's head jerked up. He turned to stare at the pipeline, far below.

Something about it had changed. The clear tubing attached to its high, arching summit no longer lay in a towering heap. The coils were unwinding like the coils of a giant snake, and the tube was sliding through the gap in the barrier and up the black, burned track, supported by hundreds of Fell End workers in yellow overalls.

The Enemy . . .

A picture drifted into Rye's mind — words appearing in the still, dark pool called Dann's Mirror, beyond the golden Door. Rye had asked where Dirk was to be found, and the pool had answered.

In the place of the Enemy

Dirk had been in the city of Oltan, in Chieftain Olt's fortress by the sea. But Olt had not been the Fellan's enemy, Rye knew that now. Olt would never have harmed the beings whose magic protected him, and Dorne, from the Lord of Shadows.

So what had the message meant by "the place of the Enemy"? Who in Oltan did the Fellan fear?

What did the Fellan fear?

Then Rye remembered. He clutched at the book beneath his shirt, gripped by a certainty that turned his bones to water. Suddenly he knew the pipeline's purpose.

The pipeline had been built to carry something far more deadly than troops, skimmers, fire, or metal. It had been built to carry the Fellan's ancient enemy into the island's heart.

Through that vast tube would come the sea — the sea, frothing and hissing, tumbling with weed and snails . . . and thick with salt.

The sea is their enemy. The salt in the water weakens their magic . . .

It would take months for Farr's troops to traverse the whole Fell Zone — to burn the tracks, to spread the metal, to spray the water pumped from the coast — the salt-laden water that would kill the Fellan's magic.

But at last, the seawater would finish what fire and metal had begun. The forest would die. The Fellan would die. The magic would die, never to rise again.

The Sorcerer Malverlain will never return to claim Dorne. Never, while we live!

The memory of those Fellan voices echoed in Rye's mind like the dread tolling of a bell.

Never . . . Never, while we live!

Rye's skin crawled. His whole body quaked. And in that instant, his mind burst through the numbing, protective wall that had grown up around it, sealing it away from the confusion and shocks of the night. Pictures began flashing before his eyes, tumbling over one another like cards thrown into the air. It was as if all the memories of his three quests beyond the Wall of Weld were coming together here on this smoky, blackened hillside.

Faene kneeling by her parents' grave in the courtyard garden in Fleet. The serene little park in Riverside. Gray guards sprawled at their ease in the Diggings . . . The pit in Olt's dungeons where Dirk and the rebels had been ambushed. The pit beneath the museum, littered with bones and belt buckles . . . Dirk in the Saltings, brandishing a dingy skimmer hook. Two boys arguing in Carryl's workroom. Pebbles cracking under the slides of Bones' loaded sled. Snail-eaten pages from Sholto's notebook . . .

A rhyme carved in stone above three Doors.

Time to choose . . .

And then Rye understood. He understood at last. There was no more struggling to force the impossible to make sense, no more need to doubt the evidence of his own eyes and ears.

He understood how it could be that Dann and his followers had fled from Olt just before the first Gifting, and he and Sonia had arrived in Oltan just before the second.

He understood why both Farr and the Fellan insisted that the Lord of Shadows had not invaded Dorne.

All he had to do was accept one astonishing fact, and everything else fell into place. And he did accept it. Why not? Eldannen, brother of Olt and Malverlain, friend of the Fellan, founder of Weld, had been a great sorcerer. Perhaps, indeed, he had been the greatest of the three.

Rye became aware that Sonia was shaking his arm. He turned to meet her frightened eyes.

"Rye, what happened?" she whispered. "You looked so strange! And your mind was moving so fast that I could not —"

"I have realized something!" Rye broke in huskily. He took a breath, deliberately calmed himself, and began to put his ideas into some sort of order, knowing that now, at least, Sonia would be able to follow him.

The Sorcerer Dann had made each of the three Doors for a different purpose.

The oldest, made of wood and brass, was an ordinary door, put in place to seal the hollow mountaintop that was to shelter Weld. The other two were powerful portals, created to serve two urgent needs.

Thinking back over what he now knew of the Sorcerer Dann, Rye felt he knew what these needs were.

Dann missed the world he had left behind. Especially he missed the forbidden forest, and the Fellan who were his mother's kin and his friends. As the years went by, his longing became so great that at last the tiled pictures he had made to remind himself of what he had lost were not enough to comfort him. Brief escapes through the wooden Door did not satisfy his need either. So much time had passed that even in the forest much had changed, and he felt like a stranger.

So he created the golden Door — a door to the past. Through it, secretly, he could leave Weld and spend time with Edelle and the other Fellan he knew well, in the forest that was still as he remembered it. He could forget, for a time, his duties as Weld's leader, his fears that his people's magic was fading inside the Wall, and his growing doubts that he had done the right thing in shutting himself away from the outside world.

"So when we went through the golden Door," Sonia breathed, "we went into the past. We traveled from the Fell Zone to the coast and back again with no idea that we were seeing Dorne as it was centuries ago — only a few years after Dann founded Weld!"

"Yes," Rye said quietly. "And we have just made the same journey, following much the same route, with no idea we had done it before."

He shrugged as Sonia gasped in disbelief. "A thousand years have passed. All the landmarks have changed so much that we did not recognize them. Vine has taken over parts of the forest. The buildings of Fell End cover land where there were only fields and a goat shelter before. The stream has been widened and deepened to make a river. Riverside has grown up on the old site of Fleet. Oltan bay has been made safe for ships to anchor close to shore. Oltan itself has been rebuilt and renamed New Nerra —"

"And the stone maze where I found you is all that remains of Olt's fortress — the part that was below the ground. The museum was built on the ruins." Sonia shook her head. "Rye, I can hardly take this in! I cannot believe we moved through the same part of Dorne twice without knowing it."

Rye wet his lips. "Not twice," he said. "Three times."

Sonia stared at him, coughing a little in the smoke haze. And slowly her face paled.

Rye nodded. His mouth was very dry. "I think Dann created the silver Door because his doubts became too much for him. He had to know . . . to know the result of his decision to leave Olt to rule Dorne unchecked. So in the space between the golden Door and the wooden one he placed a silver Door, covered with images that change depending on what is happening beyond it. The silver Door leads to exactly the same place as the other two do. But it is a Door to the future."

"The —" Sonia looked wildly around. At the rich, deep green behind her. At the blackened track stretching up toward Weld. At Fell End, the sparkling river, the rolling fields. She began shaking her head.

"You must believe it, Sonia!" The pain in Rye's chest and throat was like a knife, but he knew he had to go on. "I imagine that what Dann saw beyond the silver Door was Olt living on and on, preying on his people, becoming more cruel and monstrous by the day. What *we* saw was *our* future — the time to come after the deaths of the Fellan, after the invasion of the Lord of Shadows. We saw something that has not yet happened, but is in the making now."

"No!" Still Sonia was shaking her head, stubbornly, helplessly, as if somehow by doing that she could shake away the truth.

"Yes!" Rye said harshly. "Weld and the Fell Zone will become the Saltings, blasted to rubble, littered with metal, sour with salt, infested with sea snails that have adapted to life on land. Fell End and the surrounding farms will become the desert of the Scour. The river will dry to a pebbled track. Riverside will become the Diggings, where FitzFee's descendants will be enslaved and gray guards will roast their meat over the slab that marked Faene's parents' graves. New Nerra will be covered by the Harbor. . . ."

And, he thought but did not say, *I think Pieter, Carryl's youngest grandchild, the funny, eager boy who loves old tales, will become Bones, the hero of the failed Resistance, the half-mad wanderer in the Saltings, the clown of the Den.*

"Wait!" Sonia exclaimed, her face brightening. "Rye, you are wrong! When Sholto first went through the silver Door, he was in the Fell Zone! The *Fell Zone,* Rye, as alive and magic as it is now! He was there for a long time, and there were trees and vines and —"

"Sholto was in the Fell Zone for a long time," Rye agreed, still in that same, harsh voice. "For over a year. Then one evening the forest vanished, and he found himself in the Saltings."

"That was how it seemed to him," Sonia protested, "but —"

"That was how it *was,*" Rye cut in flatly. "Sholto was living in the future, Sonia! What happens in the future depends on what has happened in the past. And that night the past was changed in a moment . . . by the death of Olt."

All the light died from Sonia's face. She pressed her hands to her mouth.

"When Olt died, his secrets died with him," Rye went on relentlessly. "And the Lord of Shadows could start to plan . . . for this."

He waved his hand at the troops with flamers, at the clear pipe snaking up from Fell End, at the carts still dumping their loads of metal on the scorched earth, at Farr waiting on the track only a few steps away. The chieftain's words prickled in his mind.

I was well advised. . . .

Sonia took a deep, shuddering breath. Then she took her hands from her mouth, raised her chin, and tossed back her hair.

"So — we changed the distant past, and so changed the future," she said. "Well, now we are in the present, and as far as the future we saw is concerned, *this* is the past as well! So it is not too late, Rye! We still have a chance to stop that future from happening! It is not too late!"

NINE POWERS

Almost unwillingly, Rye felt Sonia's fierce determination fanning the dying embers of his hope back into life. She was right. It was still not too late to change the future, if only they could find a way. But the people of Fell End were marching up the black, burned track two by two, the giant hose pipe held between them and death drawing closer to the Fellan with every step. And Farr was moving forward, holding up his hand in greeting.

The people at the head of the line stopped dead, staring at Farr openmouthed. The people behind them pressed forward, saw what they had seen, and stopped as well. Sonia stiffened. Rye knew why. He too could feel wickedness and triumph somewhere very near.

"Keep moving!" a voice shouted.

It was Councilor Manx, his gaunt face set in a peevish scowl. Beside him was Sigrid of Gold Marsh, picking her way through the ash, a lace handkerchief held to her nose. And lumbering behind them both was Barron, coughing and very red in the face.

The astonished workers suddenly found their voices.

"Farr!" The roar was so loud that even the troops at the head of the track heard it and turned in amazement to recognize Farr's familiar figure and to cheer.

"By the stars, Farr, we thought you were dead!" Barron bellowed, mopping his streaming face. "The man Jett came stumbling into Fell End at sunrise, just as the attack began, gabbling that the Fellan had you. How did you escape?"

"Time for all that later," shouted Farr as Manx and Sigrid, both looking very startled, hurried to his side. "Have you sent the signal down the line to start the pump?"

"Not yet," Manx replied crisply. "I thought it best to wait until the hose pipe was fully in position. Two reliable men are waiting to send the flare up at our signal."

"And that is no thanks to your wife, Chieftain Farr!" Sigrid burst out, clearly unable to contain herself. "This morning she was discovered trying to persuade the soldiers we had chosen for the task to disobey their orders when the time came."

"Nearly managed to do it, too!" wheezed Barron, laboring up behind her. "Would have, if Sigrid hadn't caught her at it, by all accounts!"

251

"Two louts had helped her get to the men, it seems," Sigrid went on. "One — a great, hulking brute — was armed with a rusty reaping hook he must have taken from one of the carts. Fortunately he had been injured, as had his sly-looking accomplice, but even so it took six people to subdue them. They are both in the guardhouse awaiting questioning."

Rye's throat closed. Sonia groaned in dismay.

"Where is Janna?" snapped Farr, who had paled beneath the ash that still coated his face.

"She and her half-Fellan favorite are locked in a hut," Manx said coldly. "Jett is guarding them. He was not fit for anything else."

"It couldn't be helped, dear fellow!" Barron put in anxiously as Farr's jaw tightened. "We couldn't leave your good lady free to go around convincing the rest of the troops to defy their orders, could we? She's very persuasive when she chooses, as you well know. Her honeyed tongue could charm the bees from the hive!"

Rye's heart gave a great thud. Suddenly his face was hot, and his blood seemed to be fizzing in his veins.

Sonia swung around, her eyes wide. She had felt his jolt of excitement. She knew the idea that had come to him.

Of course!

She plunged her hand into her pocket and pulled out the bag of powers. Feverishly she unwound the string and gave the open bag to Rye.

Rye fumbled through the clutter of charms at the bottom of the bag and seized the honey sweet.

"We'll discuss this later," Farr was saying in a low, even voice that showed how rigidly he was controlling his feelings. "The important thing now is to salt as much of the forest as we can, as quickly as we can. We must only hope that the spray will be as powerful, and reach as far, as we have been told."

"It will," Manx said curtly. "We have been assured of it."

"So we have!" Barron chortled. "Everything's going like clockwork, Farr! We have those Fellan wretches on the run, for all their so-called powers. Ah, how I love to support the winning side! As I always say, there's a lot more money in it. Ha-ha — ahem!"

He turned his laughter into a cough as Sigrid shot him a disdainful look.

Rye unwrapped the little golden square and thrust it into his mouth. The taste of honey was sweet on his tongue.

"Wish me luck," he muttered. Trying not to think too hard about what he was doing, he threw back the hood and strode out of hiding.

Barron goggled, Sigrid hissed, and Manx grew very still.

Rye took a breath, but before he could speak, bellows of shock and rage erupted from the crowd supporting the hose pipe. He swayed back as a burning wave of hatred broke over him.

Then Sonia was beside him, and he could feel her strength joining his, pushing the hatred back.

The relief was intense, but Rye shook his head in frustration. He had wanted Sonia to stay in safety. He was willing to risk his own life, but not hers.

Sonia's voice whisked through his mind like a cold breeze.

My life is my own to risk, Rye of Weld! The magic will be stronger if I am with you. Besides, I have something for you. The moment I touched it I knew it for what it was. You may need it.

Rye felt her push something into his hand, recognized it, wondered for a heartbeat why she had given it to him, then saw images of Farr sitting motionless on the pipeline, Farr standing rigidly behind the tree, and understood.

The ninth power.

Again he became aware of the taste of honey, sweet and mellow, on his tongue. He pushed the melting square into his cheek and, clasping his hands together to hide what he was holding, faced the shouting people.

"Please let me speak," he said. "I have something of great importance to tell you."

And instantly, dead silence fell. Rye paused, his skin prickling. He had not raised his voice, yet somehow the people had heard him. They had heard him, they had quieted for him, and now they were waiting for him to go on.

He began, and his first words were not at all as he had planned.

"I want," he found himself saying, "to tell you a very old story — the story of three brothers."

So he told the tale of Annoltis, Malverlain, and Eldannen — Olt, Verlain, and Dann — the sorcerer sons of a Dorne chieftain and his Fellan bride. He spoke of Verlain's banishment, Olt's growing madness, and Dann's escape with his followers. And Farr and his people listened without a sound. Their eyes were fixed on him. They hung on his every word.

"Once Dann had gone, and there was no one to correct the lie," Rye said, "Olt told his people that his sorcery was all that protected Dorne from the revenge of his brother Malverlain, who in exile had become the Lord of Shadows."

He paused, and his listeners whispered fearfully, their hushed voices soft as the rustling of the trees. They all knew of the Lord of Shadows, and the name struck terror in their hearts. Plainly, however, they had not known that the ancient, evil power in the west had been born and bred in Dorne. That fact, like so many others, had been suppressed by Olt and long forgotten by a people more interested in the present and the future than in the past.

Rye saw that the councilors Manx, Sigrid, and Barron were glancing at one another, expressionless. He saw that the soldiers with the flamers and the men who had been leading the carts had all crept down the burned hill to join the crowd. He saw that Farr was staring at him intently. He felt rage and malice directed at him, but still could not locate their source.

He raised his voice a little.

"When at last Olt died and the Lord of Shadows did not invade, the people realized they had been tricked. They thought the whole tale had been a lie, and forgot it. But it had been a lie only in part. As Olt well knew, there *was* a charmed circle around Dorne, protecting it from evil invasion. But the charm was held in place by the Fellan — as it is to this day."

Again the people murmured, but this time they were frowning. They wanted to believe Rye — wanted with all their hearts to give in to the spell of his voice. Yet talk of charms and magic unsettled them, and they had grown used to thinking of the Fellan as their enemies.

"You . . . offer no proof of what you say," Farr said, plainly groping for words.

"You will have your proof," Rye replied quietly. He hoped fervently that he was right. There was not much time left. The taste of honey was still sweet in his mouth, but he could feel that the little golden square was melting away.

"The Lord of Shadows has never forgotten the oath he swore as he was banished from Dorne's shores. He vowed revenge. He vowed one day to return, to punish the people who had rejected him and to plunder Dorne's riches. But standing between him and his goal was a magic greater than his own — the protecting magic of the Fellan. So he made a plan to trick you into destroying that magic for him, and put spies among you to carry the plan out."

He took a breath. This, he knew, was the moment when his gamble would either succeed or fail. The last possible moment . . .

"The latest in that long line of traitors is with us now," he said. "It is —" He had had no idea how he was to finish that sentence, but as he had hoped and prayed, he did not have to. As the words left his lips, he felt an iron nerve break. The smoky air shimmered and thickened; there was a sudden violent scuffle; and a snarling beast with barklike hide and flaming hair leaped for him.

And in that instant, Rye's mind exploded with vivid memory. Screams of terror ringing in his ears, Sonia standing her ground by his side, he remembered at last what he had seen before the attack at Fell End. He knew who had tried to kill him on the barge, in the chieftain's lodge, in the museum. He knew his enemy.

Swiftly he raised his hands. Between them hung the faded drawstring from the little brown bag — the string of plaited Fellan hair that was Sonia's cord belt in miniature. He saw the beast's eyes blaze as it realized its danger too late. He felt Sonia's magic flow into his fingertips like prickling heat. He knew what to do.

"Be still!" he shouted, and pulled the string taut.

And the beast froze in the air and crashed to the ground, its form changing rapidly as it fell.

There was a small, sickening crack. Ash rose in a choking cloud. People were still screaming. Someone was wailing hysterically. Coughing and cursing, Farr stumbled to Rye's side.

Rye's legs were shaking so badly that he could hardly stand. He was still too shocked even to feel relief. "I promised you proof," he said, gesturing at the still figure on the ground. "Here it is."

Farr looked down. His eyes bulged.

"Barron!" he breathed. "But . . . I can't believe it! By the heavens, why would *Barron* betray —?"

Barron's eyelids fluttered. "I told you, Farr," he mumbled. "I like to support the winning side. There's a lot more money in it."

And that was all. He did not move again. Rye's throat tightened. He had not meant Barron to die. He had meant only to stop and secure him so Farr could see — so everyone could see — what he was.

"The fall killed him, Rye," Sonia said. "If he had not flown at you, he would be alive now." She looked at Farr. "Was it Barron who told you how to destroy the Fellan?" she asked abruptly.

Farr nodded, licking his dry lips. "He knew — had met — many strange people on his trading voyages. He took — he said he took — the best advice. . . ."

"The very best, it seems," Sonia said grimly.

The people who had begun crowding around them silently parted to make way for Councilors Sigrid and Manx. Sigrid was limping and her iron-gray braids hung raggedly around her shoulders. Manx was shaking all over as if he had a fever. He suddenly looked years older, and far more human.

"We cannot find Barron," he croaked. "He was right behind me when the Fellan beast attacked. I fear he has come to harm."

Sigrid snorted. "Oh, he has only run away, depend upon it," she said. "For such a fat man, he is very light on his feet. No doubt he will come strolling back any moment, red-faced and mumbling apologies for his cowardice."

"I daresay that was his plan," said Farr, and stood back so they could see the body.

Barron lay on his back, his neck twisted at an unnatural angle. He had died before his change of form was complete. One of his beefy arms was still covered with bark, the hand a hideous mass of thorny claws.

Sigrid froze. Manx choked and turned away.

Farr ran his fingers roughly through his hair. "I — I have heard of humans selling themselves to the Shadow Lord in return for magic and power. But never did I think such a thing could happen in Dorne. By the heavens, how many of the other terrors we've suffered have been Barron's work?"

"Almost all, I am sure," Rye said. "You already distrusted the Fellan. Barron made you hate and fear them. He convinced you that the slays were part of a war they were waging against you. When the time was right, he told you how to destroy Fellan magic and the Fell Zone itself. And when you hesitated, Farr, he tried to kill Zak and Janna. He knew you. He knew that far from making you draw back, those attacks would spur you on. But he protected you. He needed you."

"And if . . . if we had succeeded in carrying out our plan, the Shadow Lord would have swooped," Sigrid muttered. "Ah, Keelin, what a debt we owe you! What would have become of us?"

Rye exchanged glances with Sonia, his mind filled with chilling images. Dry, tortured land. The horrors of the Diggings and the Harbor. Desperate people, starving and enslaved. He pressed his lips together and shook his head. If he even hinted that he had seen what might have been, Farr would start doubting his sanity all over again.

They will never know what they have been spared, Rye. But we will.

Sonia's relief and thankfulness flooded into Rye's mind, sweeping the ghastly images away. *Dorne is safe,* he told himself. *Safe!* Elation rose in him, steeling him for the last great effort that lay ahead.

"We'll dismantle the pipeline," Farr said, squaring his shoulders. "We'll start at once."

"No!" Rye exclaimed.

Farr stared at him. So did everyone else, Sonia most of all.

"You are forgetting the skimmers — the slays," Rye said quietly. "The nest must be destroyed before another night comes. I will speak to the Fellan and ask if we can trespass in their territory a little longer. Meanwhile, your people can fetch some blasting powder from Fell End, and also, if you please, release the two men locked in the guardhouse. I will need their help — and Jett's help, too."

He turned to Sonia, and her eyes widened in shock as she shared the memory he had kept from her, locked away in the darkest corner of his mind, till now.

For a moment, he was back floating above the treetops in the dimness just before daybreak. He was seeing something that Farr had seen time and again, no doubt, from the Riverside watchtower. He was watching skimmers soaring to the highest point of the Fell Zone. He was watching them landing, scrabbling, fighting one another for space as they scrambled into the ragged holes and crevices of their warm, dark refuge.

Into the vine-clad cracks and caves that pocked the outer surface of the towering Wall of Weld.

THE WALL

Rye and Sonia found the Fellan waiting for them in the clearing where Dann's Mirror glimmered in the soft green light. Little needed to be said. The Fellan had understood their danger the moment they realized that Rye had been through Dann's silver Door and seen the Lord of Shadows in Dorne's future. Before that, they had thought only that the humans with whom they shared their island were breaking the treaty to gain more land. It had not occurred to them that the invaders could actually be seeking to destroy them.

"Eldannen told our sister Edelle and the others who have gone before us that Annoltis was lying to his people," said one. "Those words were passed down to us, but we thought little of them. We have been the guardians of Dorne since time began. That knowledge lives in every tree, every blade of grass, every grain of earth and sand. How could the humans here have forgotten it? It is in the very air they breathe."

"Humans are not like Fellan," said Sonia.

"So it seems. Never will we understand them."

Rye hesitated. "I think, perhaps, you used to understand them better than you do now," he said awkwardly. "For a long time, you have lived apart. Perhaps there is some knowledge that you, too, have forgotten."

The Fellan regarded him gravely. He feared he had offended them, but it seemed they were only thinking, for after a moment he felt their answer, like cool, soft wings brushing his mind.

Perhaps . . .

"There is still something we need to do," Sonia burst out, seizing the moment. "You know what it is. Will you allow it?"

As one, the Fellan smiled, and it was like the sun breaking through cloud.

"We will do more than that, little sister," a tall female said. "For the sake of our friend and kinsman Eldannen, we will rejoice."

❄

Afterward, the story of the breaking of the Wall of Weld would become legend, and the five who caused it would be called heroes. At the time, the citizens of Weld who heard a blast like a thousand thunderclaps and felt the earth tremble beneath their feet were sure their last hour had come. And those who saw Rye,

Sonia, Dirk, Sholto, and Jett appear out of thin air beside the Keep, who screamed in terror as, under Dirk's direction, Jett and Rye began attacking the base of the Wall with metal spikes and huge barbarian hammers, cursed the five as traitors.

No one could get near them to stop them. Some power prevented it. Then the first bricks fell in a shower, revealing a yawning hole, and the watchers' terror became horror, shock, and disbelief as they saw huge, pale skimmers crawling sluggishly in the cavity, flapping blindly away from the light.

The Wall that had looked so strong, on which they had all depended and for which they had sacrificed so much, was hollow. Beneath its smooth surface, all that remained of a thousand years of building was a dark honeycomb of passages and chambers, infested with the beasts that preyed on them.

"My theory is that the skimmers' first ancestors were small, harmless creatures called clinks," the dark brother Sholto was heard to call to Tallus the healer, who was watching the scene with interest. "Long ago they tunneled up through the natural rock outside, came upon softer bricks, darkness, warmth, and rats and mice — a good source of food. They bred unchecked for centuries, each new generation bigger and hungrier for warm flesh than the one before. . . ."

"And of course the more we thickened the Wall, the larger the colony could grow!" Tallus shouted, rubbing his hands and gazing at the ruined section of

Wall in fascination. "Rat numbers dwindling rapidly. Larger prey needed. Creatures start venturing out of the Wall to hunt. Those with the strongest wings feed better than the rest, so produce more young. . . . Certainly! Understood! But jell, my boy! What is this you say about *jell*?"

It seemed that the Warden's order that jell should be tidied away by being built into the Wall's ever-thickening base had caused the colony of creatures in the cavity to adapt to change very quickly. In a matter of years after the first jell went into the Wall, ferocious, strong-winged skimmers in large numbers were scrambling out into the Fell Zone night and flying over the Wall to feed.

"And why should they have looked any farther?" Sholto drawled. "For them, Weld was nothing but a giant feeding bowl."

Lisbeth of the Keep kitchens, who was weeping with joy in the arms of Crell, editor of the *Lantern*, shuddered at this, but the dark, keen-eyed young woman standing beside Tallus nodded calmly. She was a cool one, people said. Her name, it seemed, was Annocki. It was rumored that she, Crell, Lisbeth, and the beautiful, tawny-haired girl on Tallus's other side had released the old healer from the locked room where the Warden had ordered him to be imprisoned.

But the Warden, at the back of the crowd, had not noticed Tallus, Crell, Lisbeth, or the young women. His eyes were fixed on the ruined Wall, on the skimmers struggling into cover, on Rye and Sonia gliding hand in hand into the dark cavity, and moving toward the blinding light of the outside world, the skimmers' galleries crumbling to dust before them.

As the two figures reached their goal, their red hair gleaming like fire in the sun, the Warden babbled charms and crossed his fingers and his wrists. As barbarian faces peered through the deep, dusty tunnel that now yawned between the outside rock wall and the inner skin of the Wall of Weld, he cried out, against all reason, that the lighting of the city against his orders had weakened the Wall.

The plumes of the Warden's hat were drooping and stained with ink. His thin hair hung in limp strings over his sweating brow.

Appearing quickly by his side, Officer Jordan took his arm firmly, murmuring that the Warden was not well. The people tactfully looked aside as their leader was led away.

Then their eyes were caught by another sight. Rye and Sonia had returned to stand with Dirk, Jett, and Sholto. The barbarian faces had vanished from the other side of the Wall. In their place was a dim circle. The barbarians had clamped something over the hole they had blasted in the rock. It looked like a huge tube or pipe, but what it was made of no one could imagine.

Dirk and his companions showed no surprise. With a slight bow, Dirk stepped aside. Sonia moved forward, her hair flying about her head like flame. Rye moved with her, holding her hand as if somehow the link would aid her.

"Now Sonia will fill the Wall with smoke," Sholto called to Tallus, as casually as if he was discussing the weather. "It will take some time to fill the whole circle, but at last the smoke will drive all the skimmers out. Some may panic and fly straight out into the light, where they will die. Most, we hope, will escape into the feeder hose — and fly through it into the pipeline and at last into the sea."

Tallus rubbed his hands. "Excellent, my boy!" he was heard to respond. "Excellent! Now, about this substance the barbarians use to blast through solid rock. Most interesting! Do you think you could get me a sample?"

❋

As the long day of fear and wonder ended, the citizens of Weld rejoiced.

The skimmers had gone. The barbarians had retreated in peace, taking their strange pipe with them. A great sheet of metal, the like of which the people of Weld had never seen, sealed the hole in the Wall by the Keep.

The celebration was more sedate than the riotous feast going on at the same time in Fell End, but it was no less heartfelt. Beneath the glare of the lanterns that now lit the night, Weld's streets and squares were alive with music, talk, and laughter.

But as the people rejoiced, the heroes of the hour sat in the shadowy Keep kitchen amid the remains of a very welcome meal and poured out their tale to Lisbeth, Annocki, Faene, and Tallus, whose eyes grew wider with every word.

"I cannot take it in!" Annocki said, shaking her head. "There is too much to . . ." She turned to Sholto. "The ships you and Rye saw waiting at the Harbor, beyond the Door that led to the future. Did they have anything to do with the daylight skimmers — slays — at all?"

Sholto exchanged glances with Sonia, Rye, and Dirk. "We think they had everything to do with them," he said soberly. "We think they were the whole reason for the Harbor's existence. In that future —"

"The future that will now never happen," Lisbeth broke in, as if to reassure herself.

Dirk smiled at her. "That will now never happen, as you can see," he agreed, patting the rusty skimmer hook propped against his chair — the hook lost in Olt's fortress, dug up by Carryl, and carried to Fell End to be part of the war against the Fellan. "In that future, I found Father's skimmer hook in the Saltings, and later it was broken — yet here it is, as whole as it ever was!"

"We think that when Dorne was invaded and Weld was destroyed, skimmers were found in the Wall," Sonia said, far less interested in skimmer hooks than in the story. "And the Master, the Lord of Shadows, saw that he could use them as a weapon to conquer a land he dearly wanted — a place west of Dorne, across the Sea of Serpents. In Olt's time it was called the Land of Dragons, but now it is called Deltora, according to Chieftain Farr."

"My people — the people of Fleet — went there to escape from Olt," Faene put in. "Chieftain Farr told Dirk that their descendants live there still, in a city named D'Or. . . ." She had begun bravely, but at the end her voice trembled, and Dirk bent to her, murmuring comfort.

"Twice Deltora has repelled the Lord of Shadows by a magic more powerful than his own," Rye said. "We think — we cannot be certain, but we think — that when he discovered the skimmers, he realized that here were natural beasts he could use to do what sorcery, or creatures of sorcery, could not. He set about breeding skimmers that could attack winter and summer, day and night. No people could survive such an onslaught."

"And if we are right, the ships waiting at the Harbor *were* to be used to transport skimmers, as Jett said," Sonia added. "Jett was just wrong about the destination. The daylight skimmers were to be carried to Deltora so that they could bring it to its knees."

"Ha!" cried Tallus, slapping the table and making everyone jump. "So much for Weld being the center of things! Why, if what you say is true, we were only ever a detail in a far larger plan!"

"And there is comfort in that, in my opinion," Sholto drawled, smothering a yawn. "I am tired of great matters. What I need now is sleep."

Rye, Sonia, and Dirk found they agreed, and soon, despite Tallus's complaints, Lisbeth made sure that they had their wish. So as Weld rejoiced, they slept. And despite the noise beating through their open windows, despite the narrowness of their stretcher beds and the stuffy warmth of the Keep, despite the memories, hopes, and plans crowding their minds, they slept without dreams.

The waking bell did not ring the next morning, yet the Wall still swarmed with workers at the usual time. Most were heavy-eyed, but not a single man was missing. There was much to do.

When Rye, Dirk, and Sholto sat down to breakfast in the Keep kitchen, Crell and Jett were already at the table, chatting like old friends. Like the three brothers, they were both freshly bathed and dressed in the best clean clothes Lisbeth had been able to find for them. Grinning broadly, Crell passed Dirk the latest edition of the *Lantern*.

"I rushed it into print overnight," he said. "I have not had a wink of sleep. The front page will be old news to you, but look at the back!"

"The Wall is coming down!" Dirk exclaimed, scanning the smudgy print. "The layers of bricks put up since Dann's time, in any case. The foremen have all agreed. They plan to take the Wall right back to the original rock and use the rubble to fill the trench!"

"What a great project it will be!" Jett said with satisfaction, slathering a roll with honey. "And just think of the extra space for housing when the work is done!"

"And what of the jell stored in the base?" Sholto enquired with his mouth full.

"We have been discussing that," Crell said eagerly. "Jett's idea is that as the jell is taken out, little by little, it can be used for trade with the barbarians. He says they know its value, and have many goods we need."

"It will mean cutting a gateway in the rock large enough for a cart to pass through, of course," Jett put in. "But yesterday's blast has done half of that work for us. And as I was telling Crell just now, I am sure Keelin — Rye, I mean — can persuade the Fellan to allow us to keep the track to the river open. They owe him a favor."

As Dirk nodded enthusiastically, Sholto raised an eyebrow, and Rye smiled at this proof of how quickly humans, as well as skimmers, adapted to new conditions, Officer Jordan came into the kitchen. Lisbeth, looking anxious, was close behind him.

"The Warden is in the waiting room," Jordan rumbled, pulling at his mustache. "He wishes to see you — all of you — as soon as possible."

DECISIONS

The meeting in the waiting room was a strange, awkward affair. After greeting his visitors in dignified fashion, the Warden fell silent and for a long minute plucked absently at the pleats of his robe as if he had forgotten what he had intended to say.

At a nudge from Jordan, he gave a small start and cleared his throat. "Well, Volunteers," he said faintly, "I understand that one of you has earned the right to be my heir as Warden, and — ah — marry my daughter. The question is, which one?"

Lisbeth, who had insisted on being present at the meeting, silently left the room.

The Warden gazed after her vacantly.

"Crell of Southwall is not part of the contest, sir," Jordan murmured. "He was not a volunteer. He is here as the editor of the *Lantern*. I was sure you would like this important event to be widely reported."

The Warden's eyes bulged. "Oh, yes, certainly, certainly!" he mumbled. "Well, then . . ."

Jett stepped forward. "I am not part of the contest either," he said. "I did not discover the enemy of Weld. I have not won the right to be Warden."

A lump rose in Rye's throat. He wondered what it had cost Jett to say those words.

The Warden sighed fretfully. "Then it is down to you three," he said, fixing his watery gaze on Dirk, Sholto, and Rye in turn. "You are brothers, I hear. It should be easy enough for you to decide between you which one of you deserves the honor."

The waiting room door opened again, and Lisbeth strode in, with Annocki, Sonia, and Faene following. All the young women were dressed in very simple borrowed clothes. Annocki's proud, handsome face was like a fine carving. Faene's golden beauty took Rye's breath away. And Sonia . . . Sonia's green eyes were fierce and her magnificent hair seemed to light the room. Quickly, Rye looked down at his feet.

"I think," Lisbeth said firmly, "that if the Warden's daughter is to be discussed at this meeting, she and her friends should be present."

"Very good," Jordan said quickly as the Warden scowled. "Now — which one of you young men is to claim the prize?"

"Not I," Dirk said, turning to take Faene's hand. "I have my prize. And I think she will be happier outside the Wall than within it."

273

"And not I," Sholto drawled. "I am a better advisor than I am a leader — I know that much about myself. And besides, I have no wish to marry your daughter, Warden, though I respect her with all my heart. I have other plans."

Other plans.

Rye thought of nothing, and kept his eyes cast down. He did not want to look at anyone, least of all Sonia.

"Then the choice has been made," the Warden said irritably. "The third son — Rye, is it? — will be my heir." He turned to Crell. "You can announce that in the next issue of your miserable rag if you wish. And make sure to add that it is fortunate the heir is so young, because I have hopes of living a very long time!"

And at that, Rye could no longer keep silent.

He raised his head. "Warden, you cannot remain leader of Weld after this day," he said in a low voice. "If you do, I will see to it that everyone knows what I know — that your challenge to the heroes of Weld to go beyond the Wall was just a plan to rid yourself of the rebels who were threatening your power."

"How dare you!" cried the Warden, though sweat was beading his forehead, and the color was draining from his flabby cheeks.

"You knew that only the most restless young men would become volunteers," Rye went on. "And you knew that once beyond the Wall they would never return. For safety, the Sorcerer Dann made the Doors so that from the outside they only open at the touch of a bell tree stick, like this one."

He put his hand to the stick in his belt.

Someone in the room gasped. It might have been Jett or even Jordan. Rye did not turn to look. He kept his eyes on the Warden.

The Warden's mouth was opening and closing like the mouth of a fish. "You cannot possibly know —" he burst out. "That is, how do you dare to claim —?"

"I know because you tried the trick again when my brothers and I defended Tallus, the morning after the tower fell," Rye broke in. "You opened the way to the Chamber of the Doors so that we would run through it to escape from your soldiers. I daresay you locked it again as soon as you were alone."

No one spoke. The Warden seemed to shrink.

"And I know because of what I saw in a pool in the Fell Zone, the night before last," Rye went on. "The pool is called Dann's Mirror, and it holds Dann's memories — the memories he left there when he died."

Wildly, the Warden turned to Jordan, who was thoughtfully stroking his mustache. "Jordan, take me back to my room!" he gabbled. "I — I feel unwell."

"Best to stay, I think, sir," Jordan said stolidly.

"When he was very old and frail," Rye said, "Dann told his best friend and advisor that he had decided to abandon Weld. He planned to lead his people out so that the freer air of Dorne could restore their magic and they could help him rid the island of the tyrant Olt."

"Absurd!" the Warden croaked, but no one paid any attention to him. Every eye in the room was fixed on Rye.

Rye knew that it was time to finish his tale — finish it and let go of his anger. Then he could free himself from this stuffy room, free himself from the sight of the Warden, whose eyes were darting right and left like the eyes of a hunted animal.

"Dann's friend pretended to agree, but secretly thought the plan was madness. He wanted things to stay just as they were. So he persuaded Dann to take him through the golden Door, and in the Fell Zone attacked him and stole the bell tree stick. He darted back into Weld, and the Door slammed behind him. Dann could not follow without the stick, and the attack had broken his strength, so he could not go to find another. He was locked out of Weld forever."

"The same trick," Crell murmured.

"Yes," Rye said simply. "The false friend announced that Dann had died and left Weld in his care. No one thought to question him. But the secret of what really happened has been passed down from father to son in his family ever since, just as the office of Warden has."

"And when our Warden began to fear for his position, he remembered it and put it to use," Dirk said soberly.

"Indeed," Sholto drawled. "Why break the habit of a lifetime and think of something original?"

Jordan had been whispering urgently in the Warden's ear. The Warden's shoulders slumped.

"I have decided to retire," he said sulkily. "I appoint Rye of Southwall to take my place."

Rye shook his head. "Even if I wanted to be Warden, which I do not, there is someone else who deserves the prize more than I do. Without her, the quest would have failed, and my brothers and I would all be dead."

He beckoned to Sonia. She returned his gaze, expressionless, and stepped forward.

The Warden crossed his fingers and his wrists. Then, his face a picture of horrified disgust, he picked up his robes, pushed past Jordan, and scuttled from the room.

Smiling slightly, Sonia turned to Rye. "It seems the Warden does not like your idea, Rye. And I do not like it either, though I thank you for the thought. When I first began, I did not know how alive I would feel outside the Wall. My future lies there, not here."

"But — but what of Annocki!" Rye hissed.

Nocki will come with us, I hope. Her heart is set on Sholto, and I am fairly sure he feels the same.

Had Sonia not heard what Sholto had said? Bewildered, Rye shook his head at her. *Sonia, Sholto plainly said that he would not marry Annocki!*

"Sholto said that he had no wish to marry the Warden's daughter," Sonia said aloud, in a falsely casual voice that would not have deceived a child.

277

"And as I have no wish to marry *him*, though I respect him with all my heart, that is just as well."

"At last!" Annocki burst out, clapping her hands together in relief as Dirk whooped in amazement. "Oh, how I have hated this stupid charade, Sonia! How *could* you have insisted we change places?"

"It could not be helped," Sonia retorted. "At first I would rather have died than let any volunteer know who I was. And later . . . well, I did not want to spoil things."

Rye gaped at them both, feeling as if all the breath had been driven from his lungs.

"Sholto guessed long ago," Sonia added ruefully. "I do not know how."

"Mostly it was the way you snapped out orders as if you were used to being obeyed," said Sholto. And at Sonia's scowl, he burst out laughing in a way Rye had not heard him laugh for many years.

Daily editions of the *Lantern* gave the citizens of Weld much to think about over the next few days. The chieftain of the barbarians and his gracious lady had visited the city, and as a token of friendship had made the magnificent gift of a pair of iron gates to fit the new gateway being made in the Wall. The Warden had retired to a farm in the Center, due to ill health. There were to be elections for a new Warden, and it seemed that Jett of Northwall was the most popular candidate. Chieftain Farr had said that he and his people would gladly welcome visitors, and even settlers, from Weld as soon as the gateway was completed.

The heroes of the breaking of the Wall could not wait for the gateway to be completed. Much as they loved their old home, and however safe and comfortable they felt there, they had all grown used to fresher air and brighter skies.

To Dirk's and Sholto's great surprise, their mother had not only made no objection, but had announced her intention to go with them. She could visit Weld whenever she wished, she said, to visit old friends. But she liked the sound of the world outside, and would like to see it for herself.

Rye was not surprised at all. Dirk and Sholto had gone away long before Lisbeth had been forced to leave her home and seek work in the Keep. They did not realize how that had changed her.

So there came a time when Rye, Sonia, Dirk, Faene, Sholto, Annocki, and Lisbeth stood together in the Chamber of the Doors and looked up at the words engraved in the stone.

THREE MAGIC DOORS YOU HERE BEHOLD
TIME TO CHOOSE: WOOD? SILVER? GOLD?
LISTEN TO YOUR INNER VOICE
AND YOU WILL MAKE THE WISEST CHOICE.

"So — are we agreed?" Dirk asked. "We all choose the wooden Door — at least for now."

"I do, certainly," Lisbeth said firmly. "And not just for now. Chieftain Farr has told me that a house, several beehives, and a flock of goats are waiting for me at Riverside. I expect a steady stream of Weld visitors there — Tallus, for one. And Rye and Sonia, at least, need a home until — well, for a good while!"

She glanced at Sonia, who grinned. Already a strong affection was growing between them, though Lisbeth still found Sonia something of a mystery. Warmhearted Lisbeth could not understand how any young woman could bear so casually the knowledge that her own father disliked her. But in time, Rye thought, Sonia would no doubt open her heart to his mother as she had to him over the past few days. Then Lisbeth would see that though Sonia's hurt was deep, it was very old, and Sonia had found a way to live with it as she might have learned to live with any scar.

It seemed to Rye, however, that Sonia's time beyond the Wall had changed her, as it had changed him. She had discovered things about herself that she had not known before — among them the magic that, like red hair, was surely her mother's legacy. Somehow that new confidence had helped her to let much of her bitterness go.

One day, perhaps, she would even come to pity and forgive the vain, jealous, fearful man she had seen face-to-face only four or five times in her life. Perhaps she would not. But in any case, the old pain would be less in the clear air beyond the Wall.

"Annocki and I have no choice at present," Sholto was saying cheerfully. "She wants to be near Sonia, and I need to organize supplies of myrmon for Tallus, so Dorne in the present is clearly our best base. But later, perhaps . . ." His eyes strayed longingly to the silver Door.

Faene was looking at the golden Door, tears welling in her eyes. Rye's heart ached for her. How must it feel to know that your world, your time, was so far in the past? That the people you had loved had been dead for centuries, and your old home had been changed utterly?

But FitzFee's many descendants thrived on the farms around Fell End and Riverside, raising the descendants of the horses Faene had left behind her. The lady Janna's ancestors, it seemed, had been among the Fleet exiles. And Janna had promised to meet Faene at the little park in Riverside so they could stand together beneath the ancient bell tree and see what lay at its roots — the stone that bore Faene's parents' names, respected in the new town as it had been in the old.

As it happened, however, Faene's next words showed that she was not grieving for herself, but for someone else.

"I hate to think that Eldannen died in despair," she said. "He was my parents' friend and — such a good man."

"I do not think he died in despair, Faene," Sonia said, taking her hand. "He ended his days with the Fellan, who loved him. And he was certain that one day another would come to do what he could not. That is why he left his memories in the pool, and told the Fellan to keep his nine powers safe until the right person came to claim them."

Rye shrugged. "I still cannot be sure that I *was* the right person," he said, touching the little brown bag that now once again hung around his neck. "It was pure chance that I was carrying the bell tree stick. And it was pure chance that Sonia was with me when I went through the golden Door."

Dirk clapped him on the shoulder. "Right or wrong, you did well enough, little brother," he said.

"Better than well enough," drawled Sholto.

"No one could have done better," said Lisbeth.

"Rye," Sonia whispered. "Let us go! It is time! Farr and the Fellan are waiting!"

And Rye stretched out his hand and, with rising joy, opened the Door.